"WE'LL NEVER MAKE IT!"

Ed looked over his shoulder. "It looks like there are at least fifty of them."

"Don't talk!" Ki gritted. "Keep running, and, if they get within range, drop me and go on!"

"The hell with that!" Maggie cried, already gasping for breath.

If it had not been for the fact that the engineer saw them coming and after initially slowing down to stop, now was accelerating, Ki knew they'd be overtaken by the Indians.

"We've got to get up into the coal car," Ki shouted. "If we wait any longer, they'll be on top of us."

When they reached the tracks, the train's engine was almost on top of them. "Stand steady!" Ki shouted as arrows and bullets began to reach for them. "Jump for the platform that joins the two. Do it NOW!"

--◆-- **WESLEY ELLIS** --◆--

LONE STAR

AND THE
COMSTOCK CROSS FIRE

J

JOVE BOOKS, NEW YORK

LONE STAR AND THE COMSTOCK CROSS FIRE

A Jove book/published by arrangement with
the author

PRINTING HISTORY
Jove edition/February 1989

ISBN: 0-515-09925-2

Jove books are published by The Berkley Publishing Group,
200 Madison Avenue, New York, New York 10016.
The name "JOVE" and the "J" logo
are trademarks belonging to Jove Publications, Inc.

PRINTED IN THE UNITED STATES OF AMERICA

10 9 8 7 6 5 4 3 2 1

Chapter 1

Jessie stared through heavy sheets of rain at the rising Cimarron River. It was already nasty-looking water, but perhaps still fordable. She and her huge herd of Circle Star cattle had just entered Kansas, and ahead lay Abilene where she hoped to market all two thousand of her prime cross-bred cattle. But time was critical, and there had already been a lot of herds up the trail. Jessie knew that there were many more behind her. If she had to delay at this crossing for three or four days, her cattle might well become mixed with other herds, and then there would be chaos and even more delay.

Jessie looked to her foreman. Ed Wright was one of the finest cattlemen to ever come out of Texas and she trusted his judgement more than anyone's when it came to livestock. "What do you think?"

The tall, weathered Texan eased up in his stirrups, the rain funneling off the brim of his huge "The Boss of the Plains" Stetson hat. "I think it's going to be dicey, but possible for the next thirty or forty minutes. The Cimarron River is risin' about a foot an hour, and if we're going to take a swim, then I say let's do it yesterday."

"I agree," Jessie said. "Tell the men we're going in and

to keep the cattle moving. With any luck, we'll all be across within a half hour."

Ed nodded and headed into the rain. Lightning flashed and thunder clapped like giant cymbals, then rolled crazily back and forth across the heavens. The rain, which had already been coming down hard, now began to drop in bucketfuls.

Jessie pulled her slicker up tight around her neck even while realizing that keeping dry was an impossibility in this kind of weather. She would wait to go in and push the tail end of the big herd. The stragglers would need extra attention in getting across. She glanced at her samurai friend, Ki, and said, "Did it ever rain like this in the Japans?"

"Worse!" he shouted. "Have you ever heard of a typhoon?"

"A what?"

"A typhoon. It's wind and rain that blows in from the ocean to the land. Very wet and nasty. Much worse than this."

"Oh," Jessie said, knowing that her samurai would have given a much more detailed explanation if it hadn't been for the rain and thunder. Ki was the son of an American sailor and a woman of noble Japanese blood. When Ki's mother had announced her intention of marrying a foreigner, her family had been appalled. Foreigners were considered inferior people. One might be polite and indulgent enough to hold discourse or conduct business with them, but never, ever did a Japanese marry one.

But Jessie knew that Ki's mother had married her foreigner. Unfortunately, Ki's tall, handsome father had died before he could deliver his bride and his infant son to America. Ostracized by her own Japanese people, shamed and set adrift without friends, his mother had died quite young, and Ki was left to fend for himself when he was a

2

very small boy. Ki had survived, thanks to the pity and generosity of a *ronin*, a wave man or samurai who had lost his master and was now like a wave, drifting without purpose or direction. Had it not been for the *ronin* whose name Jessie could not remember, Ki would have either starved or been broken by a people who had no forgiveness or tolerance for an orphan of mixed blood.

"Jessie, if anything happens out there in the water, look for me!"

She nodded at the samurai with understanding; Ki was always the one she turned to in moments of grave danger. As she studied the man, it struck her that, even drenched and with his hair plastered down around his cheeks, Ki was very handsome. He was tall, with shoulder-length black hair secured in place with a braided leather headband. He wasn't especially muscular, but rather, he was sleek like a young lion. Sometimes Jessie wondered what it would be like to hold Ki in the night, but this could never be. He had pledged his life to protect her, and being her samurai, it was unthinkable that they should ever be lovers.

"I will," she called, "though I can probably outswim you!"

Ki took her safety too seriously to smile. He simply nodded. Jessie watched Ed Wright and the Circle Star cowboys push the leaders of her big herd toward the churning river. The cattle were bawling piteously. They had been on the trail a good long while and had crossed many rivers. But this was the worst, the last and the worst. Jessie saw the lead steer, the one named Jose with the bull-bell clanging from his brindle-colored neck, jump headlong into the current. He seemed to hang suspended above the water for the briefest moment, then Jose was swimming hard. The cowboys looked worried, but they trusted Ed Wright. So they drove the other cattle in right behind Jose.

3

There was some hesitation at first, but then they followed right in and formed a long wavering line as they struggled across the Cimarron.

Jessie was pleased. The herd was swimming strongly, and Jose was already clamboring up on the northern bank, shaking himself free of water. It was going to be all right. She pushed into the river towards the rear of the herd. Ki stayed close to her but not so close as to crowd her. He was not a cowboy, but at times like this, he simply emulated what the others were doing and was quite valuable.

The water was surprisingly cold to Jessie. It felt as if it were snow-melt, and it numbed the lower part of her legs and filled her boots. Her palomino horse, Sun, was long-legged and could swim well. It went at the current without fear. Like her own cowboys, Jessie used her rope to keep swatting at the cattle in order to keep them bunched closely together. That way, they stayed on a true heading. Singly, it sometimes happened that the current spun them around, made them disoriented and set them off swimming in the wrong direction.

"Tree in the water!" a voice cried. "Tree in the water!"

To a cowboy mounted in mid-river, there was no more terrifying announcement. During heavy rains, it was common for riverbank trees to have their roots torn away and then to crash into the current only to be swept downriver. To have a ton or two of timber come rolling down at you while a thousand head or more of terror-filled cattle went crazy was to know the meaning of big troubles.

Jessie looked upriver and saw the tree rushing down on them. It was right in the center of the river and coming very fast. A big cottonwood, its trunk was at least forty feet long and as wide around as the barrel of a draft horse. And worse yet, every single one of its hundreds of limbs and tiny branches would grab and snarl a swimmer as if it were covered with fishooks—only instead of dragging its catch up, it would drag it down.

Jessie was not a woman who panicked, but as the tree swept in on them, she believed that she as well as the men and the animals at the drag end of the herd were sure to die. At least most of the men and cattle were already safely on the north bank.

The tree seemed to gain speed as it grew nearer, though Jessie knew that it was an optical illusion. The cattle nearest to the approaching menace saw it first and they tried to reverse directions. But it was too late for them, it was too late for anything but to trust to luck, God and the samurai.

Ki shouted, "On your saddle, Jessie. Stand on your saddle!"

Jessie stared in amazement as the samurai stood up in his own saddle. Not full up, but crouched with his feet planted firmly in the seat. And then, she understood. Ki was not about to allow the tree to sweep over them, he was going to leap over or at least on top of it!

Two other cowboys nearby also understood. They acted as quickly as Jessie. When the tree churned and ripped into the swimming herd, pulling cattle down into the depths of the river, Jessie crouched on her saddle and then jumped for the trunk.

She caught it and hung for a second, feeling the power of the water make the tree shiver as its lower branches raked the riverbottom. Ki was at her side in an instant. He pulled her upright and then he grabbed another cowboy and helped drag the man onto the tree trunk.

Jessie saw watery visions of cattle crashing crazily under the river's surface, pinned by branches and the strong current. Her horse was gone and she thought Sun had drowned until she looked upriver and saw the palomino struggling on the rest of the way to the north bank.

5

"We lost Vince," Ki said. "Vince didn't jump and the tree went right over the top of him and his horse."

The other cowboy clung to the branches. His name was Pete and he was as pale as a headstone. "Same's gonna happen to us, I think. Ain't no way that we can ride this river all the way down to the Gulf of Mexico. Sooner or later, the under-pinning of this sonofabitch is going to be torn way and then she'll turn over and over like a rollin' pin."

"He's right," Jessie said. "We can't stay for long. And the water is too swift to swim for shore."

"As long as we're alive, we have hope," the samurai told them very calmly.

His pronouncement was followed by a deafening volley of thunder and a blinding show of lightning. "Maybe God just said, 'piss on that'!" the cowboy cried.

Jessie stayed near Ki. She could see her cowboys galloping headlong down the northern riverbank to catch up with the tree. At their lead, Ed Wright was shaking out his rope though she could not imagine what he intended to do with it. "He sure can't do anything but hope to get himself dragged in with us," she said.

"Don't be so sure," Ki answered. "Your men are very determined when it comes to keeping their boss alive. Almost as determined as I am."

Ed Wright was riding a fast bay, a powerful animal that quickly drew abreast of the floating tree. The Circle Star foreman was shouting something but with the rain and thunder, it was impossible to hear. Suddenly, four or five other cowboys joined Ed, and then they all seemed to draw into a huddle.

"What the hell are they doin', Miss Starbuck?"

"I think," Jessie replied, "yes, they're tying their ropes

6

end to end. Ed is about to throw us a loop and pull us in."

"No," the samurai said.

"What do you mean, 'no'," Pete said. "Of course they are! It's the only goddamn chance we got!"

"We'd be towed under the minute we jumped," Ki said, shooting a hard glance at the young cowboy who dared to use profanity in Jessie's presence and who seemed to be on the verge of panic. "The current or the underwater branches would drag us under. All they'd pull up would be three drowned bodies."

"Well I'll take my chances with them over nothing!" Pete shouted.

"Ki is right," Jessie said to the young cowboy in a calm voice. "You stay."

"Bullshit!" Pete was almost out of control. "Unless you got a better idea then I don't see why—"

He didn't finish speaking. Ki stepped forward. Suddenly his hand darted out and its rock-hard edge caught Pete with a *tegatana* blow against the base of the neck. The young cowboy sagged, but Ki grabbed him before he toppled into the Cimarron. Ki looked up at Jessie and though he said nothing, his expression was quite explicit as to its meaning.

"If we live through this, I'll pay him off in Abilene and send him on his way," Jessie told the samurai. "I can't have a man who'll crack under pressure and disobey my orders."

The samurai nodded. His eyes never left Ed Wright who was now forcing his mount into the churning river. Instead of tying his rope to his saddlehorn as he would when roping cattle, the end was now tied to another man's rope and that to another and another. On the bank, ten cowboys were now ready and every one of them seemed to be

7

shouting either encouragement or instructions as the big cottonwood surged downriver.

Ed went as close to the tree as he dared, and then he began to twirl his rope. But it wasn't easy atop a swimming, plunging horse in a hard rain. The rope must have weighed as much as mine cable because when Ed threw it, it fell ten yards short of the tree's roots.

Ki showed no hesitation as he went after the rope. His lean, limber body cut the water like the blade of a knife and vanished for so long that Jessie's hand moved involuntarily to her mouth, and she was sure that he had drowned. But instead, he shot through the surface with the rope in his teeth. With powerful strokes he swam back and slapped the loop around a massive tree root. Grabbing it, he motioned for Ed and the cowboys to pull.

Apparently, the cowboys had also thought that they'd only be dragging three humans to shore, not an entire tree. But Ed Wright saw at once that Ki was correct. So, he made a circular motion with his hand and reversed his horse. A few minutes later, he and every available cowboy on the trail drive was dallied to the long rope stretching out into the Cimarron. And though it took them nearly a mile to bring that tree into shore, they were finally successful.

"Is he hurt bad?" Ed asked, looking at Pete.

"No," Ki said.

"What happened? I couldn't see very well through the rain, but it almost looked to me as if you—"

"He was hit on the head," Jessie said, making it sound as if Pete had slipped and fallen. She did not want any of the other cowboys to know that Pete had lost his nerve. Such a thing could haunt a man the rest of his life. Maybe next time, Pete would retain his composure in a moment of great stress. But when it happened, he wouldn't be on Circle Star's payroll.

Jessie paid the best, and she demanded the best. In this line of work, anything less would most likely get you killed.

Chapter 2

Abilene lay steaming in the sun. Its weathered grey boards cracked and hissed as the rain water evaporated. For twenty miles in all directions around the town, thousands of Texas longhorn cattle bawled in hunger as they rustled what had once been tall prairie grass.

"Fer cripsakes!" a cowboy groused. "I never seen so danged many cattle before in my life!"

"And they all look like they're starvin' to death," another observed. "Why, there ain't enough grass out there to feed a small flock of constipated grasshoppers!"

"That's enough of that kind of talk around Miss Starbuck!" Ed Wright warned in a hard voice.

"It's all right," Jessie said, bringing Sun to a standstill and letting her eyes take in the discouraging sight. "I've never seen so many cattle either. Why, even the loading pens at the freight yard are full."

"Wonder what they're feeding them cattle," a cowboy asked. "But what I really want to know, is where's all the trains and cattle cars?"

"That's the million dollar question, all right," Jessie mused aloud. "And it's the first one I'll ask. Ed, stay with the herd. Move 'em however far out you have to in order to find good feed. I won't have my cattle getting thin while waiting on any railroad. And you can bet the cattle buyers are loving this plenty. They watch the cattle lose weight, and then just before they're loaded, they weight them and make their offers by the pound. We've worked too hard to bring this cattle up from Texas in good market condition. I'll not let us be cheated now."

The men nodded with understanding. They knew that Jessie was one of the wealthiest women in the world. That her father, Alex Starbuck, had left her with a fortune in assets in the form of giant companies located on nearly every continent. But what they really admired about their female boss next to her splendid good looks, was that she ranched as if it was important, as if her livelihood depended upon the productivity of her Circle Star Ranch. Her cowboys were the best. There wasn't a one of them that would have worked for some "hobbiest" as they derisively termed some of the rich British and easterners who came to the West and bought ranches for show. No sir! Jessie was dead serious about the importance of making a profit at ranching, and the men who worked for her would not have had things any other way. Ranchin' was serious, it wasn't no children's game.

Jessie and Ki rode into Abilene, and on their way, they passed through a sea of cattle. She recognized many of the brands from all over Texas and guessed that there was about three weeks worth of herds lined-up waiting on the railroad. She was also recognized by many cattlemen and ranchers. The Circle Star was one of Texas's most prominent spreads. When old Jake Waters reined his big dapple mare around and trotted out to greet her, Jessie waited, knowing that she could trust old Jake to tell her the truth of things.

"Jessie Starbuck, my God! You jest get prettier year

11

after year. It's good to see you, girl! I jest wish it was on better days."

Jessie reached out and shook the cattleman's calloused paw. Jake was in his sixties, though he worked and looked like a man considerably younger. He also shook hands with Ki. "Good to see you again, too, samurai. I can see you're doin' your job and keeping the best thing old Alex ever did happy."

"I try," Ki said, a little overwhelmed by the man's sheer exuberance in the face of such an obviously discouraging situation.

"What's going on, Jake?"

"Jessie, you ain't heard yet?"

"No, we just arrived."

"The Kansas Pacific Railroad got washed out three weeks ago. They been having so much rain here lately that the damned thing keeps washing out over and over. They'll get a train or two in and out, then it stops again. Everyone here is about to go crazy."

"Don't go crazy, Jake. Go somewhere else."

"Sounds easy. Seems to make sense. Only it ain't and it don't."

"Why not?"

"Because the damn washout is at the Republican River. Ain't nothin' movin' east on this line."

"If I have to, I'll drive my herd all the way north to Wyoming or Montana."

"You do that, and you'll just find that they're ranges are already overstocked. The last damn thing they want or need is Texas cattle. Those days are over."

Jessie was getting angry. Not at Jake, not at anything she could put her finger on in a hurry, but angry all the same. "All right, then that leaves the West. I'll take them west."

Jake shook his head, "You know Denver town is no good for beef right now. Wyoming has been dumping their beef down that way for years. No profit in throwing bad money after good, Jessie."

"So what do you advise, Jake? Shall we all shoot ourselves or should we shoot the herds first . . . and then ourselves?"

Jake managed a weak grin. "Leave your pistol in your holster, Jessie. There's cattle buyers coming around to see you. They're still buying everything that comes up the trail."

Jessie's green eyes sparked. "I'll bet. They expect everyone coming in here to see the same damned sight that I did—an ocean of starving cattle. So how much leverage has a rancher got with that staring him in the face? What are they offering, Jake? Tell me what they paid you?"

"They offered me two cents a pound," the old rancher said quietly.

"Two cents!" Jessie said in a stunned voice. "They ought to be arrested for cattle rustling. Jake, most of the cattle I've seen can't weigh over eight hundred pounds. That means you're getting just sixteen dollars a head. Tops. And every day you wait for the train, you're probably losing another two to four bits a head. Why, you could wind up owing *them* money?"

"The price drops a quarter a cent each pound for each week that you wait," Jake added.

Jessie placed her hands on her shapely hips. She was dressed in a man's riding clothes, and there was a gun resting on her hip. She could use it and was ready to use it on the first cattle buyer who came along and told her that her cattle were worth little more than she could have gotten for them down in Texas without lifting a finger to drive them to the nearest railhead.

13

"Jake, are you trying to tell me that all the buyers are working together this year? That there is no competition? It's just a 'take it or leave it' deal because you have no other choice?"

Jake nodded. "I'm afraid that's the way of it. A rich woman like you can leave it. But I'm a small rancher, like many of the others here. I can't afford to go back owing money. I got a crew to feed and wages to pay. I got expenses that have been waiting for six months for this herd money. I got to go back home with something or I'm finished."

Jessie's voice softened. "How many cattle did you bring up this year?"

"About eight hundred."

"Have you signed anything yet?"

"No, but—"

"Then don't sign," Jessie said. "Right now, I'll pay you twenty dollars a head."

"Now, Jessie. I ain't no charity case," Jake protested. "Just because I once saved your daddy's life, don't mean I expect any repayment."

"You saved my father's life?"

"It's a well-kept secret," Jake confided. "I didn't mean to mention it, though. Just slip of the tongue. Just a slip."

Jessie threw her head back and laughed out loud. "Why you slick old dog, you've probably been waiting for twenty years to use this one on me, haven't you?"

"But it's the God's truth! I did save your pa's life! 'Course, we was all alone that day, so there was no witnesses. But I remember it as if it was yesterday. There was thirty, no at least forty Comanche, and they was—"

"Stop it, you old conniver!" Jessie cried. "All right, I'll pay you twenty-one dollars a head and that means you

14

earned an extra eight hundred dollars for saving my father's life."

"He was worth a lot of money even way back then," Jake said with a wink of the eye. "But I'll gladly take payment. Cash would be nice."

Jessie nodded. "Meet me in front of the Bank of Kansas in an hour and you'll have your money, Jake."

"God bless you, beauty! And if you want to buy any more cattle, I can get them for you at that same price."

"I'll bet you can," Jessie said. "No, unless you find someone that you can trust and knows how to keep his mouth shut. I need fewer cattle, not more of them. And right now, I'm not even sure what I'm going to do with my own herd, let alone yours. But I'll find a way to make a profit or my last name isn't Starbuck."

Jake waved. He looked ten years younger than he had a few minutes earlier. He was grinning so broadly that his face appeared as if it were ready to break. "I'm sure you'll think of something!" he called. "Your daddy always did!"

Jessie did not go to the bank first, but instead to the telegraph office where she intended to wire her ranch headquarters and to check and see if her people had sent any messages. When you are responsible for thousands of employees around the world, something always seems to be going wrong, and so Jessie tried to keep in contact by telegraph when expediency was required. When she entered the office, it was pretty busy with the cattle buyers sending messages to their slaughterhouses back east. Everyone was tense and the mood was dark.

"If they don't get that damned railroad trestle fixed over the Republican River, we might wind up eating every damned head of cattle we've bought!" a buyer groused.

Jessie's answer was succinct, "Then you'd be eating the

15

cheapest Texas beef you've ever put a knife and fork to, Mister. Two cents a pound is an outrageous price."

Every cattle buyer in the office stared at her. The man she had been speaking to said, "You must be the renowned Jessica Starbuck." His eyes slid up and down her length. "Well, well. So you're not impressed, huh?"

"Not a bit." She looked at the buyers. "So don't waste your time in coming around unless you're willing to pay at least double. I won't sell a steer for less than thirty dollars. Not a one."

"Maybe you haven't heard about the Republican River and the problems all cattle ranchers are facing. It's what is now being called a 'buyer's market', Miss Starbuck. It might change into a 'seller's market' some day, but that day is a long time coming."

The telegraph operator had just finished sending a message and now was rapidly thumbing through a stack of telegrams. "Miss Starbuck? I got one here that sounded pretty urgent when it came over the line yesterday. You better take a look."

Jessie stepped forward, the cattle buyers were immediately forgotten. "Thank you," she said as she walked over to a corner of the office and slowly began to read the message which was from her ranch headquarters.

DEAR JESSIE. MESSAGE RECEIVED FROM A GRANT SAWYER FROM VIRGINIA CITY, NEVADA. MARKED URGENT. MRS. SARAH SAWYER MURDERED. NEED YOU AND KI OR WILL NOT SURVIVE. PLEASE COME AT ONCE IF POSSIBLE.

Jessie stared at the telegraph. Sarah had been one of her oldest and dearest childhood friends. They had grown up together and spent many a happy day riding and playing out on the range. Sarah had married Grant, and it had been a wonderful marriage. One made in heaven. Jessie could

16

only imagine how badly Grant's heart must be broken over the loss of his beloved wife. Of course she would come to Virginia City! And what vile kind of man or men would murder an innocent woman like poor Sarah or threaten Grant, who was a hardworking mining man?

Jessie looked up from the telegram, the shock of its message only starting to bring out the real deep pain and loss she knew would last for a long time. "This is all?"

"Yeah," the operator said. "That's every word."

"Thanks." Jessie opened the door and stepped outside where Ki was waiting. He took one look at her and knew there was trouble.

"What is it?"

She handed him the telegram.

Ki frowned and said, "So now we have two big problems. How to sell almost three thousand head of cattle and how to help Sawyer. I liked Sarah very much. She was a kind and generous woman. I hope the man who killed her has already been hung."

"It doesn't sound as though he has, does it? I mean, Grant says his life is in danger. That leads me to the conclusion that whoever killed Sarah is still a threat."

Ki agreed. "That line of logic could be extended to a further conclusion that there is more than one person involved in the threat. A gang or some kind of an outlaw band."

"But what did Grant and Sarah have that anyone would want? They were just barely scraping a living out of that mining claim on the Comstock."

"Mining claims have a way of going from worthless rock to fortune," Ki pointed out to her. "It can happen at the single strike of a pick."

"Yes. That's true enough. At any rate, we have to find out."

"So we're going to Nevada?"

"Of course."

"What about those three thousand head of cattle?"

Jessie did not hesitate. "The answer came to me in a moment of inspiration. We'll take them with us and sell them on the Comstock. That's how we'll kill two birds with one stone. We'll not only help poor Sawyer, but we'll help ourselves. And you just wait and see if we still don't make a profit before all this is over!"

Ki had no doubt that she would make a profit despite what would be a high freight charge. Of course, they'd have to drive the herd a couple of hundred miles on up to the Platte River where they could be loaded aboard the Union Pacific Railroad. The Union Pacific would take them as far as Ogden, Utah where they would change for a Central Pacific train.

Jessie took a couple of steps and then stopped and said, "I'm going to go back in there and wire my bank to send this bank a chunk of money, Ki. Enough not only to pay off Jake Waters, but also to pay that big freight bill we'll have to come up with to satisfy the Union and Central Pacific Railroads."

"You're accountants will never even notice the expense," Ki said.

"They'd better." Jessie leaned in close. "But the thing of it is, I'd like to send the message without those vultures inside knowing about it. Can you think of a way to get them out of there quick?"

"I guess I can," Ki said.

"Then I'd be grateful if you'd please do it."

Ki shrugged his shoulders. He stepped into the telegraph office and yelled, "Hoof and mouth disease. Someone's found hoof and mouth disease and it's breaking out in all the herds!"

The cattle buyers, many of whom had already spent thousands in expectation of a big profit when the railroad was finally repaired, suddenly saw visions of entire herds toppling over to die on the prairie. In a panic, they all shot out the door and raced down the street running as hard as they could.

Ki smiled, he extended his arm in a sweeping motion. "The telegraph office is all yours, Miss Starbuck."

"That was very cruel," she told him, trying not to smile. "But also quite brilliant."

Ki just nodded his head. He knew that she was right and that a response was entirely unnecessary.

Chapter 3

Jessie and Ki rode swiftly out to their herd, which Ed Wright had finally bedded down about five miles from town. She dismounted and faced the expectant cowboys. What she had to tell them would not be good news. They'd been on the trail for months now and they were ready to tree the town, get drunk, laid and carouse all the meanness out of their systems.

"Boys," she said, "gather around because I have something I have to tell you. I've bought old Jake Water's herd of eight hundred. They'll be joining our herd tomorrow and we're pushing the whole bunch of them on to the Union Pacific Railroad."

Jessie saw the disappointment in their eyes. "You men have worked mighty hard in getting our herd this far north, but a couple of hundred miles more isn't going to kill you. As I'm sure you've guessed, there's just no market here in Abilene until after the trains are running. And by then, there will be tens of thousands of longhorn cattle here and still no market. So we're taking them to market at Plum Creek where I feel sure they have big holding pens and plenty of feed and water. Any questions?"

A cowboy pulled off his hat and rolled its brim. "Miss

Starbuck. I don't suppose you'd give some of us a little advance on our wages and let us go into town tonight? We're mighty thirsty and it's been... I mean, I ain't touched nothing but horse and cowhide fer..."

"Goddamnit!" Ed groused. "Of course you ain't getting paid yet! The drive isn't over, is it?"

"No, but... well, what the hell are we supposed to do with our money in a place called Plum Creek?!"

"That's for you to figure out when you get there. Besides, a fool can always find ways to spend his money, no matter where he is!"

The cowboys all laughed and the issue was settled. Jessie allowed her foreman to make the day-to-day working decisions regarding the cattle and the men. But she made all the big ones.

Ed looked at her. "After we get to the Union Pacific, where are we shipping them? Back east to Chicago?"

"Nope." Jessie addressed Ed, but she was really speaking to them all. "We're going to load the cattle and ship them to Reno, then drive to the Comstock Lode and sell them to all those miners up in Virginia and Silver City. I know the area is booming, and when men have money in their pocket, they always want meat and whiskey."

The cowboys nodded with grins on their faces. "We all going to Nevada, Miss Starbuck?"

"No need for that. Once the cattle are loaded, I'll need only a couple of men to help me get them down to the Carson Valley. They'll need feeding and watering on the train, but that will also require just a few hands. I'll decide who goes back to Texas and who comes along to Nevada when we get to the railhead. I imagine most of you boys would rather go home."

They nodded. Probably none of them had been this far from home except on previous trail drives. Texas cowboys

21

did not like to stray far from home, and when they did, they seemed to make it a point to return as soon as possible.

Ed Wright said, "I hear that the Union Pacific is still having fits with the Sioux and Cheyenne up north. We're going to have to be careful, Jessie."

"I know that. But I also know we have to act now. So it's up early in the morning and I expect Jake's cattle to be here early. I told Jake I wanted to leave before noon."

"It would interest us, given that we couldn't give a steer away within a hundred miles of here, why you bought old Jake's cattle?" someone asked. "They're just straight longhorns like all the others."

"Because Jake is an old friend and because I intend to earn a nice profit on every single head we ship to Reno. I telegraphed the Union Pacific and I know exactly what the freight and feed charges will be to destination. They're high."

A cowboy grinned. "So what'd you do, get mad and buy their whole derned railroad so you could send 'em free?"

Everyone had a good laugh about that and Jessie joined them. "I guess my father and I have been known to do things like that," she said. "But not this time. The Union Pacific is not for sale or it might have entered my mind. No, we'll pay the same charges as anyone else, but I'm still banking we can deliver these cattle to the Comstock Lode fat and healthy. And that we'll get top dollar and make a profit. It all depends on you."

The smiles died. Jessie continued. "There has been Indian trouble north of here. Quite a bit of it. So I want every man to keep a sharp watch, and once we get started, we'll be keeping a double night watch."

The cowboys groaned. The riding and the eating dust

was hard, but not having enough sleep was the thing that hurt the most.

"I'm sorry. But that's the way it'll be. I have been assured that there will be enough railroad cars waiting for us at Plum Creek on the siding by the pens. So take the evening off with just a skeleton crew on watch. We push north tomorrow."

That was it. The cowboys weren't pleased and, in fact, were purely disappointed in not being able to go into Abilene and raise hell. But their spirits would rise in the morning. Once the sun came up and the herd started moving, they would be fine. Despite any words they might tell you to the contrary, a cowboy was always happiest in the saddle.

"Hey!" one of a crowd of mounted Texans yelled. It was early morning, and they had gathered just outside the Circle Star camp as Jake's herd was being delivered. "I got cattle for sale any day for two cents a pound! Hell, yes, I do!"

Jessie ignored the man and his friends as she finished her breakfast. They were small-time cattlemen who had caught wind of Jessie's generous offer. Just how they'd learned the details was something that Jessie did not want to consider. Knowing Jake, she figured he'd probably gotten drunk and told everyone in Abilene, and that's why they were out here right now trying to sell her their herds for more than the local cattle buyers were paying. Jessie had already told the heckling riders that she was not in the market for either their company or their offers.

"Hey, Miss Starbuck," a rough-looking man yelled. "I got a thousand head and I'll let you have them for a cent and a half a pound! That's a better deal than you got from Jake. What do you say!"

"They're worth more than that. Find a better market!" she called to the riders.

"Can we follow you up the Union Pacific and get a 'special rate,' the kind of rate that rich folks get?"

Ki was close to Jessie and he started to turn his horse and ride out to the hecklers. But Jessie stopped him. "Let it be," she said. "They're upset and jealous. They figure their cattle are as good as Jake's, and they need the money about as bad."

"The fact that you were generous to an old family friend should be considered a reason for admiration, not ridicule," the samurai said with an edge in his voice. "I won't let them taunt you with insults."

"And they haven't been."

But just then, one of the twenty or so riders yelled, "Listen Miss Starbuck, why don't you get your fancy ass . . ."

He didn't finish. The words just died in his mouth as Ki and the entire Circle Star crew charged him and the others. Jessie sat back and watched. The numbers were about even but she knew the contest was a mismatch. Ki alone was worth four or five men, and her riders were tough and madder than hell.

She watched Ki knock the foul-mouthed one right over the back of his horse. Then the rest of her crew threw themselves off their mounts, and the battle was on. There was so much dust that all she could do was hear the grunts and the thudding of fists against flesh. It must have been a hell of a brawl. Horses scattered in all directions. Now and then, a man would come hurtling out of the dust-cloud only to pick himself up and charge back into the melee.

When the dust finally cleared, it was Ki and the Circle Star men who were standing. Jessie was pleased. She nodded and then smiled widely in appreciation of her crew for upholding the honor of her good name.

"Get your horses and let's ride!" she shouted.

The Circle Star riders slapped the dust off themselves, wiped their bloody noses and knuckles off and went after their horses.

It was a good crew. One of the best.

They pushed straight north out of Abilene, tasting the grassy-sweet wind in their faces and feeling the sun warm their clothing. Ahead lay miles and miles of untamed country. You could still see an occasional buffalo on the horizon but they were rare, and Jessie knew that the days of the Indian were nearing their end. The buffalo migration, which had been repeating itself according to the changes of season, was finished. The railroads with their steel ribbons had cut off the buffalo trails and brought hide hunters. The last Indian warriors were still out on the plains, but most Indians were now on reservations. Unfortunately, those that remained free were turning more and more to raiding ranches and eating beef. There were so few buffalo left that they could not survive on what had been the staple of their diet for centuries. It was not easy for an entire race of people to change their life-style. The Indians were nomadic plainsmen, hunters, not farmers or settlers. She wondered if they would ever change and accept the harsh policies established for them by the rigid Bureau of Indian Affairs.

For two days, they saw nothing but waving grass. There was not even a tree and that told Jessie they were in Nebraska. "Do you like the country?" she asked her foreman one afternoon as they plodded along in front of the cattle.

"Me?"

Jessie smiled. "We're the only ones out here besides Ki, and I know he hates flat country."

"Well so do I," Ed told her. "I don't like lots of mountains either. But a man could go crazy out here with nothing but flat ground to look at. As green and as flat as this country is, it musta been God's intention to use this country for a snooker table when he finished making the rest of the world."

"And do you think he did?"

Ed jeust shrugged. "If he did, he sure didn't mis-que 'cause there isn't so much as a rip in the earth to break things up. It looks to me like we ought to have left it to the buffalo and the Indians."

"It's good for growing things." Jessie looked down at the tall grass and the rich, dark soil. "The day will come when all of this will be covered with corn or some other crop. It will stretch as far as the eye can see."

"And what will they use for water?"

"The rain," she said. "That and wells. I got a feeling this isn't like southern Texas. You wouldn't have to dig that deep to find water."

"Probably wouldn't taste all that good even if you found it."

Jessie smiled. Ed was a fourth generation Texan, and though he liked Colorado, he didn't have much use for any other state or territory. "I'll be sending you back with most all of the boys," she told him.

"I figured as much. There's a lot of work left to be done back at Circle Star. But I'm worried about you and that telegram you got from Nevada. Sounds as if things are pretty bad on the Comstock."

"Yes, it does."

"Sarah Sawyer was a fine girl. I 'member how you and her used to play together when you weren't much bigger than mites. I 'member how your pa and I put you on ponies and you'd race all over the yard, scatterin' the layin' hens

26

and raising the dust so bad it'd turn the hanging laundry gray on the washlines. You and Sarah were like sisters."

"I'll find out why she was murdered," Jessie vowed. "If the man that did it isn't in jail facing a hanging, I'll make sure that he soon will be."

"You jest be careful," Ed drawled. "I ain't never been to Nevada, but from what I hear, it's not much good. Too damn wild."

"Texas is pretty wild too," Jessie reminded her foreman.

"Used to be. Tamed down some the last few years. The Comanche and the Kiowa don't raid much anymore. Haven't seen an Apache on the ranch for bettern' two years now. Things is getting almost citified out there on your range."

Jessie snorted. Ed was being ridiculous on purpose just to get a reaction. She'd not give him the satisfaction of one, though. Circle Star was still being raided by Indians, whites and Mexicans for its cattle and horses. There were still gunfights in the towns and rope justice out on the ranges. Maybe not as many as in the past, but enough so that no one would think of riding the range unarmed.

Jessie stood up in her stirrups and scanned the horizon. "If we see another creek like the one that we found this morning, I want to make camp. This heat will pull the fat off my cattle pretty quick and there's no telling just where and when we'll find more water."

"That's for sure," Ed told her. "We're sort of blazing new trail here. I just hope what we heard about Indians doesn't prove to be true."

"I expect it was. I plan to double the guard and to tell them to watch out for sneaky Indians who savor the taste of cattle. I'll be glad when we reach Plum Creek and load these cattle. Once loaded, I can relax, knowing they'll be taken care of by the men."

Ed Wright shook his head. He was in his forties and almost a father-figure to Jessie since Alex had died. "That's where you're dead wrong," he warned. "The only time you can ever let your guard down is when the money traveling from your hand to that of your local banker is already safely deposited in his burglar-proof vault. And even then you have to worry."

"About what?"

"That your banker doesn't turn into another Jesse James."

Chapter 4

The samurai awoke before dawn and lay still on his blankets for several minutes before he rose silently to his feet. He stood and watched the Circle Star herd, noticing that they were beginning to rise and graze in the twilight emerging from the east. Four Circle Star cowboys rode around and around the cattle, singing or humming to themselves. Outside of the cowboys, their horses and the cows, nothing moved.

Ki walked to a small stream and knelt beside its cool water. He bathed his torso and then his face. The cold night air and the water were refreshing. He walked back to the sleeping camp and pulled on his *ninja* costume, a close fitting black suit with a hood that covered his head except for an eye slit. Only Ki did not pull the hood over his head but instead collected his bow and arrows.

The samurai ran off to the north, over the ground that the herd would be covering in a few hours. A cowboy saw him and waved, but the samurai did not wave back. It was Ki's custom to go off early in the morning alone. If he saw an antelope, he would shoot it for meat because it was the understood law that a cowboy did not eat his own beef on its way to market. Ki could have taken his own horse, but he preferred to run, to condition himself. His stride was long and smooth, and the cowboy he left far behind with the Circle Star herd continued to watch Ki until his silhouette disappeared over the distant horizon. It was a pretty sight to see a man, or any creature for that matter, run as gracefully as the samurai. And even though it was against their code to walk when they could ride, there was not a man on the Circle Star payroll who did not envy the samurai for his gracefulness and his ability to hunt with that crazy-shaped bow he carried. There was also, they agreed, something a little terrifying about a man who raced the morning sunrise wearing a hooded black suit.

Ki ran on and on, his breathing light and his stride smooth and steady. He knew that the land was not flat at all but fell off to the east and rose to the north. Somewhere up ahead was the Platte River and the railroad, but between that place and this, there were Indians. Ki could feel their presence, and so he kept his eyes moving, always searching.

He saw spotted antelope on a slight rise of land. They were grazing under the dying stars. Ki stopped and fell softly to the earth knowing he was lucky to be downwind of the wary creatures. He began to move forward like a *ninja*. A *ninja* trained in the art of invisible assassination. Old Kobi-san had always taught Ki to use whatever cover there was to conceal his presence. Never mind that there was almost no cover on a Nebraska prairie. The grass was just a few inches deep, and what rocks there were could not have hid a sage hen.

Ki used the land's flatness to its best advantage. He stayed low to the earth, moving through the grass with surprising quickness as he drew closer and closer to the little band of pronghorn antelope. Once, the buck threw his head up in the air as the wind shifted for a moment. Ki froze. The buck tested the wind but lost the samurai's scent. The animal's keen eyesight missed nothing as it surveyed the prairie all around it. Sensing no danger, the buck continued grazing even as the samurai crept forward, his hand reaching around behind his back to pull an arrow out of his quiver. He nocked the arrow without even bothering to look at it. Antelope would be a welcome change from rabbit and sage hen. If he could kill two or three, then he would be able to supply enough meat for the camp for several days.

Ki was still over a hundred yards from the grazing antelope, and though he felt he could hit the buck, he knew that he would only have one shot at this distance before the fleet antelope were up and running away. He decided that he would attempt to get closer. It was excellent *ninja* training, and Ki believed that the antelope would test his stealth far better than any human. He moved slower now because the buck was very alert. The buck stopped grazing, raised his head, and flicked his tail nervously. Ki was disappointed in himself. He had thought that he would get within fifty yards before the antelope first sensed danger. How...

His thoughts were interrupted as the antelope suddenly bolted and raced directly at him. Ki's arm drew the bowstring back behind his ear. He was just about to release his arrow when he realized that something had scared the antelope. Ki threw himself into the grass, and the antelope blazed past him just as four mounted Indians surged over the low hill and came flying after the antelope. The last Indian was riding double and Ki saw at once that he held a white woman captive. She was riding in front of the warrior and was thus a shield.

Ki lay still, but one of the Indian's ponies spotted him lying down and spooked. It's rider's full attention had been focused on the fleeing antelope. Like his two companions, the Indian had an arrow nocked in his bowstring, and though he knew they could not hope to overtake the antelope, they would possibly wear them down. Ten years before, the Cheyenne hunters would not have given antelope a moment's glance. They'd have hunted buffalo instead, but now they were reduced to doing far more hunting for much less meat.

When the racing Indian pony spooked and threw its rider off balance, it was almost on top of Ki. The samurai knew there was no longer any point in trying to hide. He stood up in full view of the Cheyenne and waited to see what they intended to do. Sometimes they would attack, sometimes not.

The Cheyenne attacked. They probably knew that there was a herd of cattle within the sound of a rifle's shot, so they did not use their carbines. Instead they drew knives or raised their terrible war lances and came at the samurai. Ki stood his ground. Bow already nocked, he set his feet and without appearing to even aim, he drew the bowstring back to his ear and fired. The bow turned 180 degrees in his hand, and the arrow, the one Ki called "death song," sang like a warbling canary as it streaked to its target. Only when the small ceramic bulb, which lay just behind the arrowhead, exploded deep within the Cheyenne's chest did the shrill warbling die—like the Indian who somersaulted over the back of his mount.

The second Cheyenne had been unnerved by "death song" and the queer bow that fired the shrieking arrow. The warrior's lance, tipped with feathers, drew back in his hand as he leaned forward on his horse. With a gutteral cry, he hurled the lance. The throw was almost perfect. The samurai had to step sideways, and even then the lance flicked at the black ninja costume. Ki dropped his bow. His hand

32

darted inside the ninja tunic and withdrew a star blade. He spun as the horse flew past him, and though slightly off balance, he hurled the shuriken blade with deadly force. It struck the Cheyenne in the side of the neck. The man screamed and then toppled brokenly from his racing horse.

The third Cheyenne threw caution to the wind. He no longer cared about the sound of gunfire. He drew his carbine and jumped to the ground. His momentum carried him forward and he rolled, bringing the rifle up to his shoulder. Ki was on top of him. They struggled with the rifle, and it exploded between them, burning both men with black powder. The warrior was strong and desperate as they struggled for possession of the rifle. Ki heard the white woman scream a warning, then looked up just in time to see the last Indian yank a Navy Colt out of his sash and open fire. Ki spun his opponent around and the bullet intended for him struck the Cheyenne locked in his arms. The warrior's eyes widened, and he stiffened in surprise and death. Ki dropped the man and threw himself sideways as another pistol ball came his way. The samurai reached for another shuriken blade but the Cheyenne and the woman captive were already retreating.

Ki wanted to save the white woman, and he suspected that there were many more Cheyenne nearby making it imperative that he overtake the Indian before he reached the main Cheyenne raiding party.

Ki snatched up his bow and arrows, then managed to grab the trailing horsehair rope of an Indian pony. It was not the one he would have chosen first but a smaller, weaker animal that did not look very fast. Still, it was the only one of the three that did not run away. He vaulted onto its back and used his knees to turn the scrubby beast and send it in pursuit of the warrior and the woman.

"Come on, run!" he yelled at the pony who laid its ears

back and bucked each time he gave it a whack across the rump. "Run!"

The pony was a disaster. It was old and had the roughest gait of any animal Ki had even ridden. Every stride caused his testicles to smash into the little beast's withers, and the pain was excruciating. The scruffy brute kept stumbling, and Ki thought it was going to fall a dozen times. But because the warrior he chased was riding double and the woman was struggling, Ki actually discovered that he was gaining on the pair. He lifted his bow and reached over his shoulder to yank out an arrow. The Cheyenne's back was a broad target, and Ki thought that he could kill the man with a little luck, despite the jarring agony he was being subjected to. Ignoring the pain in his groin, Ki nocked an arrow and drew his bowstring. The fleeing Cheyenne warrior was still a good forty yards away when the samurai fired and saw his arrow streak forward. Unfortunately, the white woman used that instant to slam her captor in the ribs and almost unhorse him. The Cheyenne was forced to throw himself sideways in order to avoid falling, and Ki's arrow just missed its target.

The Cheyenne saw and heard the samurai arrow pass close beside his body. He must have realized that he was as good as a dead man if he did not get rid of the woman and flee for his life. So he drew his knife and slashed at her. She howled as the blade cut her arm, missing her breast. The woman fainted and fell. Her body struck the prairie grass, and she rolled over and over before coming to a stop. Ki pulled the Indian pony to a painful standstill and weakly tumbled to the woman's side. The pony raced away after the fleeing Indian; it bucked and squealed in a show of great displeasure.

"Are you all right!" Ki said, kneeling beside the unconscious woman. She was younger and much prettier than he had expected. Most of the white women taken hostage were the wives of farmers, hard-faced women with deep lines and thick, calloused hands. Not so this beauty. She was yellow-haired and fair, though she had lost her bonnet and her face was burned raw by wind and sun.

Ki made a very quick examination. The woman seemed all right. Her pulse was strong and steady, and she was breathing normally. He used a strip of her dress to bind the wound on her arm. When it stopped bleeding, the samurai slung his bow over his shoulder and picked the young woman up. She was full-bodied, yet he carried her as easily as he might a child.

Ki hurried across the prairie knowing that his and the woman's survival very likely depended on who reached them first—Jessie and the Circle Star crew, who would have heard the shots that were fired, or the rest of the Cheyenne. The samurai kept his eyes straight ahead as he jogged. The bold sun lifted off the eastern horizon and glared redly at him. Sweat rolled off his torso, and his breath began to quicken.

He glanced back over his shoulder when he passed a slight rise of land, and what he saw brought a shiver of dread. There were at least thirty Cheyenne warriors on his backtrail, and they were racing their ponies after him. If he were caught, there would be no mercy, not with three of their number dead.

Ki heard the Cheyenne's howls of rage and shock as the warriors came upon their three dead tribesmen. The samurai pushed his speed up to a full run, though every muscle of his body was under great strain. Far in the distance, he saw the Circle Star herd and the Texans racing their horses out to help save him. Ki did not think that they would be able to reach him and the woman in time, but when he glanced back and saw the Cheyenne still at the sight of the death-battle, he changed his mind.

Then, the Cheyenne really began to howl as they leapt onto their ponies and came in full pursuit. They were too late. Jessie and her cowboys reached the samurai first. There were no words necessary as the Texan's dismounted and cooly formed a battle line.

"Hold your fire until I say so!" Jessie yelled.

The Texans did as ordered. The Cheyenne drew their rifles, but when Jessie fired and their leader was swept from his horse, the Indians wisely peeled off to both sides.

"They're going straight for the herd!" Ed Wright shouted.

The cowboys were swinging onto their mounts and racing back toward the herd that was being held by only a few of their number. But Jessie was flying after the Cheyenne, her big palomino horse gobbling up the distance in great, swinging strides.

Her first and by far greatest concern was for the three cowboys she had ordered to stay behind and protect the herd from danger. I should have left more, she thought, raging at herself as she raced after the Indians. I should have left more!

The Indians were only a half mile ahead of her but they might as well have been ten miles for all she could do to stop them. They hit Jessie's three thousand cattle like a storm of hornets, scattering them in all directions. There was gunfire, and Jessie saw a cowboy named Bob take a bullet in the shoulder and then fall under the stampeding cattle. The Cheyenne were killing beef just as earnestly as they were going after the three cowboys. Jessie saw one drive his war lance through a big brindle steer's neck. The animal crashed to the earth kicking and bawling in its death throes.

36

Jessie and her cowboys came flying in on the Cheyenne firing their guns. But the Indians had done this before, and they scattered like the herd. In minutes, they were putting distance between themselves and the angry Texans, but Jessie knew that the damage had already been done. The Cheyenne had, in just that single devastating attack, managed to slaughter at least twenty beeves. They would return once the Texans rounded up the herd and been obliged to move it on toward the Platte River.

"Smart," Jessie said, as she raised her pistol and fired it over and over in a signal for the Circle Star cowboys to gather the herd and bring it back to camp. "How is he?"

"Bob must have more lives than a damned cat," Ed Wright said. "I thought he was a goner for sure, but he managed to survive somehow. He's shot and trampled but he says he's ready to get back on his horse."

"The hell with that noise," Jessie said, relief flooding through her. "Patch him up and toss him in supply wagon. We're pushing on north to the railhead at Plum Creek. It seems we've traded a white woman for about twenty head of cattle. I guess that's fair enough. No other men hurt?"

"Not that I could see," Ed told her. "Considering how hairy things looked just a few minutes ago, we came off amazingly well. But it sure galls me to think of leaving those murderin' Indians all that beef."

"They're hungry, Ed. All their people are hungry. I just wish they'd have saved us all this trouble and asked for some beeves. I'd have gladly given them twenty to avoid bloodshed and to pass across their hunting grounds."

Jessie galloped back to see Ki and the woman. "You want to tell me what happened?"

Ki told her.

"And you've no idea who the poor woman is?"

"Not until she wakes up," Ki said.

Jessie dismounted with her canteen. She handed it to Ki saying, "I'll have the chuck wagon up here in a few minutes. She can ride with old Shorty Taylor. Until then, you stay right with her. She's probably been through hell, and if she remembers that you were the one that saved her, that's going to loom mighty important in her mind."

"Her face is blistered by the sun and the wind," Ki said.

Jessie gave Ki her own Stetson. "Shield her with this. I can get another someplace." Jessie climbed back on her horse. She shook out her long, strawberry blonde hair, which was beautiful. Next to her, the yellow-haired woman looked downright plain. "Don't leave her for even a minute, Ki."

Ki nodded. He was concerned because he certainly did not want to "loom" big in any woman's mind but he understood what Jessie was saying. He watched her ride off, then uncorked the canteen and splashed some water on the palm of his hand. He cradled the woman's head in his lap and patted her face with cool water.

The young woman's eyes opened, and Ki saw a moment of fear. Probably, it was because of his own dark skin or his long black hair and headband. But then, recognition came into the woman's eyes and she relaxed. "You're the man that saved my life."

"I helped you escape."

"Not just escape," she said, her voice a whisper, "you saved me from them. My name is Maggie Linker and I have been praying for someone like you for three weeks."

Ki tried to hide his surprise. "You were their captive for that long?"

"Yes."

"We'll try to get you back among your people," he said, wanting to reassure her.

"I don't have anyone. I was traveling alone on a stage-

38

coach when they attacked and killed everyone."

"But you must have someone."

"No. I was going West to work in a Virginia City dancehall. I thought it sounded like fun, and there was an advertisement in the paper. I was raised as an orphan."

"Oh."

Ki started to scoot away from her but she grabbed him, her eyes suddenly betraying that she was still afraid. "Will those Indians ever come back?" she asked him, her voice nearly frantic.

"I don't know," the samurai told her. "But I think not. They were probably more interested in beef than in trading bullets."

The woman pushed herself up and then threw her arms around the samurai. "I saw everything you did. I couldn't believe it, and yet you were the answer to all my prayers."

Ki swallowed noisily. The woman clung to him. He raised his hand and stroked her yellow hair. "You've been through hell," he said. "We'll make sure you get to civilization and that you never have to go through this again."

She began to cry. Just a few sniffles at first, then big, racking sobs. She clung to Ki so hard that he was amazed at the strength of her arms.

A long time passed, and he could hear the cowboys coming up with herd. Jessie's voice turned him about. "Is she going to be all right?" she asked with great concern.

Ki nodded in the affirmative. "She's just going to need a little time."

Jessie agreed. Time and, apparently, the undivided attention of her samurai. "You better join her and Shorty in the chuck wagon. We've spread some blankets behind the driver's seat. You can lay her in there out of the sun."

Ki glanced over at the chuck wagon. Like most trail cooks, Shorty was cantankerous and mostly a man who stayed to his own thoughts. He'd not be pleased about this new arrangement. To hell with him, Ki thought. "Can you stand, Miss Linker?"

"If you help me."

A cowboy chortled, but Ki shut him off with a dark glance. He helped the woman to her feet and then helped her up into the wagon. She would not let loose of his hand.

Ki eased down on the blankets and closed his eyes. "Let's roll 'em," he said.

"Always knew you was a worthless sumbitch!" Shorty spat. He slapped the mules hard and the wagon lurched forward.

The yellow-haired girl clung to the samurai and looked deep into his eyes. "I want to know everything there is to know about you," she told him.

Ki grinned. Something told him that the last leg of this trail drive was going to be the best.

Chapter 5

It was sometime in the wee hours of the morning when Ki heard a thump on the bed of the chuck wagon and then his name being called, "Ki?"

The samurai opened his eyes. He was sleeping under the chuck wagon, a condition that was not to his liking but was the best possible compromise.

Maggie was hissing loudly down through the floor-boards of the chuck wagon. "Are you awake?"

"No," the samurai said. "Go to sleep."

"I can't."

"You're going to wake someone up." Ki peered through the darkness toward the cook who was sleeping at the other end of his wagon. "Probably Shorty."

"No I won't," she argued. "Not if you come up in the wagon so I don't have to talk so loud."

Ki frowned. "You'd better go back to sleep, Maggie. We got a long, hard day to the railhead."

"But that's what I want to talk to you about."

Ki considered his options. He could either try to ignore Maggie and hope she went back to sleep, or he could get up and join her for a minute and put an end to this non-sense.

"Ki!"

"All right. I'm coming up. Just keep your voice down or you'll wake up the whole camp."

"Okay."

Ki slipped out from under the chuck wagon. It had rained earlier in the night, and everything was wet. He sprang up to the wagon seat and then eased into the dark interior of the wagon. No doubt, Maggie needed some reassuring about what they intended to do with her once they reached Plum Creek.

"Ki," she whispered. "We're going to go to Nevada together, aren't we?"

"Sure. I told you we'd take you on to the Comstock Lode which is where we're going."

She sighed and laid her head on his chest. "I just needed to hear you say that again. You're the only one that I can trust, Ki."

"You can trust Miss Starbuck," he protested.

"I meant the only man."

"Oh." Ki jumped back a little. "Hey, what are you doing!"

"Shhh!" she was almost giggling. "You know what I'm doing."

Ki did know. She had slipped her hands under his loose-fitting pajamas and she wasn't trying to scratch his back. "I think you'd better not," he said, pulling her hands away.

"Why!" He could not see her clearly in the dark interior of the wagon, but from the tone of her voice, it was obvious that she was amazed. "Don't you like me? Or is it Miss Starbuck? That's it! You love her. Admit it!"

"Sure I love her, but not like you're thinking. We're like brother and sister."

"Prove it to me."

42

"Now wait a minute," Ki said. "I don't have to prove anything."

"You're right," Maggie said, with disappointment. "But just touch me right here and say you don't want me and . . . and if you can do that, I'll let you go back to sleep."

Before Ki could quite believe what was happening, she had his hand and was slipping it up against the generous mound of her breast. It was incredibly soft and he could feel the beating of her heart. Desire flooded through the samurai. He did not take his hand away but rubbed the breast gently and then took the nipple between his thumb and forefinger and rolled it. He heard her gasp, and her hands touched his body again.

"Is it so wrong for a woman who was used like a bitch in heat to want to make love to the man who saved her life? To want to cleanse herself from three weeks of hell and degradation with something good? I need you, Ki. I've had men before, but I never needed men. There is a big difference."

Ki understood. He pushed her down, and he kissed her mouth, ears, throat and eyes, feeling her shudder with expectancy. His hand worked its way across her turgid nipples and then slipped down to her abdomen and lower, resting on her soft mound of womanhood.

"Oh, Ki," she whimpered, "I need it from you so bad. But I may be hurt a little inside. Be gentle."

The samurai nodded for he knew that this woman had been used hard by the Indians. The wonder of it was that she could still want a man. It made him humble to think that she wanted him to cleanse away the nightmare she had endured.

She lay back, breathing hard, her legs parting as his fingers begin to explore her treasure. His fingers slipped inside of her, and she arched her back and began to rotate her hips. She was going to be all right. He could feel her growing damp as she tried to pull him onto her. Ki took her hand and guided it to his long, thickening shaft. A tiny moan escaped her lips as she encircled his great rod with her fingers. She gripped it gently at first, then harder as her own passion mounted.

His lips dropped to her breasts again, and he teased her nipples with his teeth. Maggie's stroking of his erection became more energetic, and her fingers worked from the root of him to the tip, her thumb hard on the sensitive head of his manhood.

She lifted her knees, and he eased up and lowered himself down between her silken thighs. He could feel her tugging frantically at him, trying to draw him inside of her. Ki hunched his hips forward a little and felt the head of his shaft enter her warm wetness. He held his body as rigid as a piece of steel, and she groaned with anticipation.

"What are you trying to do to me," she pleaded. "Don't make me suffer or beg for it!"

Ki took mercy on her and rocked his hips forward hard. His long tool drove up into her yielding body, and her mouth flew open. He covered her mouth with his own and felt her hands scrabble across his back as his own fingers played with the bud of her desire until she moaned. The chuck wagon started rocking, and some of Shorty's pots and pans began to slam around in the chuck box. Ki realized he was going to awaken the entire camp if he didn't quit fooling around and get this over with in a hurry.

"Ohh, ohhh, yes!" Maggie wheezed as she lost control of her body and began to pitch and buck. Outside, the coffee pot fell off the counter and banged loudly on the ground, but Ki did not care. He was losing his own control and pistoning his huge root in and out of Maggie. Suddenly, his muscled body went stiff, and he filled the woman with torrents of his seed.

They both collapsed, gasping and shuddering with the afterglow of their lovemaking.

"Goddamn," Shorty breathed hoarsely from down below them. "Goddamn you samurai, it's hell to be old!"

Maggie clamped her hand over her mouth and began to giggle. Ki just smiled. Maybe some day he would be old, and a younger man would make love to a woman very close to him—where he could hear everything, imagine everything, remember how it had been. If that happened, Ki would remember Shorty and he would forgive.

They swam the Platte River, which was low this time of year. There had been no more trouble with the Cheyenne, and they all breathed a little sigh of relief when they saw the Union Pacific Railroad tracks shining like ribbons of silver in the afternoon sun.

"Which way do you figure we are from Plum Creek?" Ed Wright asked Jessie, who had been across America on the transcontinental railroad more times than all the rest of them put together.

"It's to the west," she decided. "I'm pretty sure of it."

Ed made a signal, and the cattle herd was turned west. The longhorns and crossbreds were so trail-broke that they almost looked for the drover's signal and then followed it before a command could even be made.

Jessie glanced back at the chuck wagon as it pulled out of the river. She saw Maggie Linker and smiled. That girl had sure recovered in a hurry from her ordeal. She never wanted to talk about what she had gone through, and that was fine. Jessie knew what Maggie had endured, and she was proud of the young woman for standing up to it and holding her head high. Many a white woman rescued from

45

Indians had gone half-crazy or, at best, considered themselves ruined for any decent man. Maggie had no such damaging self-image. Ki had probably done wonders for her in the darkness, and Jessie was grateful, though the girl seemed to occupy an enormous amount of the samurai's time and energy.

They trailed the herd on all afternoon, and by early evening, they could just see the water tower at Plum Creek Station. "I'm glad I was right," Jessie said. "The last thing we need would be to have gone in the wrong direction."

Ed nodded. "We'd have just hit another station twenty or thirty miles along."

"I know that," Jessie said, "but this is the one that is supposed to have the cattle cars waiting on the sidings for us to load."

"Don't see no cattle cars."

As they drew nearer and nearer, Jessie's spirits continued to droop. In truth, it quickly became obvious that there were no cattle cars. In fact, it seemed to her that there had been a depot at Plum Creek but she could not be certain. There were hundreds of little stations across the nearly two thousand miles of transcontinental railroad stretching between Omaha and Sacramento. Some stations became settlements, then trading posts and even sizable towns. Rock Springs, Laramie and Cheyenne were all big towns that had started as stations. But others never got much past the depot stage. Maybe they were too far from water, or the soil wouldn't support agriculture. Or, in the case of Plum Creek, they were squarely in the middle of Indian territory and the climate was distinctly unhealthy.

"Damn!" Jessie slammed her fist down on her saddlehorn. "I don't see any cattle cars waiting on the siding either! Come on, Ed! Let's go find out what the hell went wrong this time."

Jessie and her foreman rode ahead of the herd, and when they were within a mile of isolated railhead, it was clear that Plum Creek had been hit by the Indians and burned out. There were cattle cars on the siding all right, but they were no more than blackened wheels and rolling gear without sidings or even flooring. The train depot and its loading platform was also nothing but a pile of ashes. From all appearances, the Indians had even tried to burn the corrals and loading chutes, but by the time they'd attempted that, they'd been bored and had given up and ridden away. The only thing that appeared undamaged was the leaky water tank.

"What are we going to do now?" Ed asked her as they galloped nearer.

The faint stench of death reached Jessie's nostrils, and she steeled herself for what she knew she would see. "I don't know," she admitted.

They tied their horses to the water tower and walked over to what had been the depot. Near the door, a half-burned corpse lay covered by soot. It held what was left of a gun in it's skeletal fist. Jessie walked through the ruins and found the telegraph key. She lifted it from the ashes, and the burned wires led her toward a telegraph pole. "Ki knows Morse Code. He can send a telegraph back to Omaha and tell them what happened here. He can ask for a new bunch of cattle cars."

Ed nodded. He stared at the corpse. "That poor devil didn't have a chance out here alone. But maybe he had time to send a message to the nearest station."

"Maybe." Jessie sort of doubted it though. The Indians understood about the talking wires, and they would have been smart enough to have cut the wires before the man could have sent a message. She could not imagine how awful and alone this telegraph operator must have felt during the last few minutes of his life. She hoped he had not been tortured.

Jessie shook her head. "Could be we should have gone after those Indians. They might have been the same ones that attacked and burned down this station."

"That's impossible to say," Ed told her. "Indians have been raiding and hunting across this land for centuries. They've got to hate this railroad for what it's done to their buffalo herds. Cut 'em right in half. Brought too damn many people. My guess is that the Indians that did this were not the same ones who attacked our herd last week."

"Thanks," Jessie said. "I guess it doesn't matter now much anyway. The best thing we can do is to get that message off and just try to get our herd out of here as soon as possible."

Ki arrived, and it seemed obvious to him that he needed to take the telegraph key and shinney up the pole to send a message. The ground wires were either burned away or broken by hooves. So he climbed the pole, respliced the wires to the telegrapher's keys and tapped out an urgent message to the Union Pacific headquarters in Omaha. He was very slow and deliberate, but made few mistakes. He told the Union Pacific the condition of Plum Station and its hapless telegraph operator. He asked for more cattle cars to be sent at once. Then, he sat back and waited for a reply.

It took a half hour in coming, but when it did, Ki was ready with a paper and pencil. From down on the ground, Jessie, Maggie and Ed Wright watched anxiously until the telegraph died and Ki tapped out a sign off.

"What do they say!"

Ki dropped the little sheet of paper, and it fluttered down to Jessie who read it quickly before crying, "They're out of all cattle cars between Salt Lake City and Omaha! That's ridiculous!"

"Shall I send that message?" the samurai called down from his perch high above them.

"Yes!"

Ki sent the message to Omaha. A few minutes later, he had his reply in a single word. "Sorry."

"Damn!" Jessie raged as she began to pace back and forth with her hands on her shapely hips. "Here we are, stuck a million miles from nowhere with the country crawling with Indians, and there's no cattle cars waiting and none on the way."

"We might be able to fix the cars," Ki said from high above. "There's a lot of trees along the Platte. We could cut new sides and beds. Nothing could have hurt the rolling gear or the wheels."

Jessie looked up suddenly. "Ki, you're brilliant! Telegraph Omaha and tell them we have to get this herd to Reno. Tell them to send some locomotives. Enough to pull the cattle cars. Tell them I intend to deduct the cost of repairs from their damned exorbitant freight charges!"

Ki grinned down at her. "Anything else?"

"Yes!"

"What?"

Jessie smiled. "As soon as you're finished playing monkey in the tree-top, get down and give us a hand. We've some axes in the wagon, but there must be some more axeheads, hammers, saws and nails in this sea of ashes. Help us find them so we can make new handles. Oh yes, one more thing, ask them when the train will be here!"

"Yes, ma'am," the samurai told her as his fingers began to tap out Jessie's new message on the fire-blackened telegraph key.

Ki slid down the pole. "They said a train has already pulled out and will be here in 48 hours. The problem is, it will have passengers, and it can't wait and throw off the entire railroad schedule for cattle."

"That sure doesn't give us much of a chance,"Jessie said. She looked at the samurai. "Can we do it?"

"We have no choice," Ki said. "Not unless we don't mind waiting around here for another week until the next train passes through."

"I mind a lot," Jessie said with conviction. "We all mind. So let's get moving. There is a lot of work to do!"

The Circle Star cowboys did not need to be told. They'd have to work forty-eight hours straight, but there was not one who complained. What they wanted most was to get the herd safely on the cattle cars and moving to market. What they wanted second most was to get their horses turned south and head back to Texas.

Ed Wright started barking orders. Men jumped off their horses and into the ashes. Every station kept a good supply of tools on hand. Some were to repair the track, but there would also be axes and saws to cut firewood in winter and an occasional railroad tie that needed replacing.

"I found an axehead!" a cowboy shouted. "Over here! This must have been the toolbox. There's all kinds of stuff, but every damn one of them has the handles burnt clean off."

Ki grabbed an axehead. "I'll start on the handles."

Jessie watched him hurry away with Maggie Linker in tow. Ki would put both himself and that woman to work, and they'd soon have handles on every tool that was found. Jessie looked at the herd, which seemed so large, and then at the line of sideless cattle cars. "We sure got our work cut out for us this time," she said to herself as she started for the cottonwood trees along the river. "But I'd bet grasshoppers against gold that we can do it!"

Chapter 6

It was hard and rugged work cutting lumber and then hauling it to Plum Creek and trying to build adequate siding and flooring for the railroad cars. Fortunately, the carriages themselves had steel corner braces. The crew used the braces to attach solid posts to all four corners. Once the corner posts were in place, it was a simple matter to fasten branches and poles between them.

Ed Wright took charge of the construction, and Jessie stepped aside. Ed was everywhere shouting orders. When the first cattle car was repaired, the cowboys could see what was expected, and they worked in pairs, each competing to see who could finish the most cars.

"They look like nothing more than pole corrals on wheels," Jessie commented to her foreman. "Do you think they'll hold the cattle?"

Ed nodded. "If we have time, we'll fill in the lower sides so they can't step through. But as for the burned off sliding doors, we'll just use a rope gate. Them cattle are going to eat a lot of smoke and soot, but they sure won't be lacking for air."

Jessie was a little concerned. "Are there enough cars?"

"Yeah, but we'll have to pack 'em together pretty tight."

Ed removed his Stetson and wiped his brow with his sleeve. "The thing that I'm worried about is if the damned Union Pacific sent enough locomotives to pull this many cattle."

"I'd better send Ki back up the pole and make sure," Jessie said.

A few minutes later, Ki tapped out another telegram. He waited several more minutes and then received a reply. "They say they don't have enough locomotive power for that many cattle."

"What!" Ed shouted. "Tell them they damn sure better find an extra locomotive, because we ain't leaving cattle and we ain't driving them another foot."

Ki again tapped out the message. But the reply came back the same. "They say there is no way they can pull three thousand head. Half will have to wait until the next train comes through."

"When will that be!" Jessie called.

Ki already knew the answer. "A week. They said it will be a week."

"Aw, for cripessakes!" Ed shouted.

Jessie drew a deep breath and let it out slowly. "There is no help for it," she said. "It'll give us a little more time to do a better job on the cattle cars than we send out in the first bunch. Ed, you and the boys will have to stay here with the herd for an extra week."

Jessie took a deep breath. What she had to say next was not going to be well received by the samurai. "Ki, there may be hundreds of Cheyenne out there. Ed and the boys need your eyes to alert them against a surprise attack. I'll have to ask you to say here with the herd and come along in a week."

The samurai had slid down the telegraph pole to stand before her, and now he was upset. She saw the protest rise in his expression but such was his control that it passed almost at once, and he nodded his head. "As you wish, Jessie."

"It's not as I wish at all. But I'd never forgive myself if this crew was attacked and wiped out. If you see a huge war party, one that is too large to defeat, I want you to warn Ed, and then every single man is to leave. Miss Linker, you had better accompany me to Reno."

"No," she said moving in close to the samurai. "Not yet. Not until Ki comes too."

Ki was embarrassed but his voice was firm. "I want you to go with Jessie," he said. "It will be safer."

"I don't care! *You* saved my life, not her. I can use a rifle. If there's an attack, then I want to help fight off the Cheyenne. I owe them something back."

Jessie knew that she could not take Miss Linker with her kicking and screaming. "You're a very brave woman. I just hope that you have not made a very foolish, even fatal mistake."

The samurai lifted his chin. "She will not fall into their hands again," he promised.

Ed Wright had his mind on another matter. One very close to his heart. "I could never just abandon the herd," he said. "You know that a cowboy will fight to the death before he'd do that."

Jessie was firm on this. "A cowboy—as well as a ranch foreman—also obeys orders, Ed. There are only sixteen of you, including Ki and Miss Linker. That's not nearly enough to stand up to a huge war party. And I'd rather have you all alive and lose a hundred thousand cattle. I can buy cattle anytime I want. I can't buy your lives back if you get overrun and scalped."

Ed, Ki and the others just stared at her in stony silence. They'd follow her orders, but only as a last resort. The

53

idea of leaving half the herd to Indians was almost incomprehensible.

Ki glanced out at the flat country. "I would humbly ask you one thing," he said. "Do not go to Virginia City until I can join you."

"I can't do that," Jessie said. "Sarah has been murdered. I have to go to see Grant at once. But I will promise you this. I'll stay out of trouble until you are at my side."

Ki did not seem especially relieved. He'd seen her get in and out of bad scrapes more times than he cared to remember.

Ed looked at her, his face troubled. "What about the cattle after you arrive in Reno?"

"I'll hire a few men to drive them down towards the Comstock Lode."

Ed did not look pleased. "I guess there really isn't any choice, is there?"

"None at all," Jessie told him. "I'm sorry it had to work out this way. At the next station, I'll send a few wires out to the United States Army asking for the protection of you and my cattle. But don't count on their help. The Army is stretched mighty thin on the northern frontier."

"Our men know how to fight," Ed told her. "Only difference up here in Nebraska is that these are Cheyenne instead of Comanche or Kiowa. And instead of sagebrush, we have grass. But blood and bullets don't change. Fighting is still fighting."

He was right. Jessie looked at the herd. "We've got a lot of work cut out for us even to load half the Circle Star herd."

During the next twenty-four hours, Ki worked like a man possessed, and early the next morning, he climbed the pole when he heard the telegraph key clicking. Jessie hurried over to look up at him. "What do they say now?"

"They want us to have the herd loaded and waiting on the side railing when the train arrives this afternoon."

"Loaded!" Jessie cried. "What do they think we are! How are we supposed to load fifteen hundred head of cattle without a locomotive to pull the cars?"

"It can be done," Ki said. "We have enough men and horses to load each car as it's completed, then pull them one at a time down the rails. There is a slight downhill grade between the loading chute and what's left of the depot."

"All right," Jessie said. "Then that's the way we'll go about it." Jessie looked at her pocket watch. "What time is the train due?"

"In about ten hours," Ki said.

"Good. We'll keep the cattle on graze until three hours before it's time to load. Then we move and we move fast."

The cattle cars were ready. Jessie watched as cowboys roped the front coupling and pulled the first creaking car down to the loading chute. It was easy enough work for just two mounted cowboys to pull one empty car, and never had she seen such a strange-looking cattle car. It looked like a traveling ketch pen with its green branches and poles all hung together by wire, what nails they could find in the ashes, and rope. Jessie was not at all sure that the siding would hold up to the long trip to Reno. They would have to climb over South Pass and the Wasatch Mountains, then descend into the Great Salt Lake Basin. From there, the rickety cattle cars needed to withstand the blistering, dry heat of the Humbolt Sink and the deserts of Nevada.

"Take heart," Ed told her as if he could read her dark thoughts. "I guarantee you these cars will hold our cattle until they get to the Sierras. I'm just damn glad they won't have to face something like Donner Summit."

55

"So am I," Jessie said. She watched as the first cattle were pushed up the chute and into the first car. A few of the more irascible longhorns tested the siding with their long, sharp horns. Jessie watched apprehensively as they hooked and stabbed at the fresh cottonwood poles. The poles held, and the cattle stood and bawled with displeasure. They did not like the new flooring, and they wanted back on the Nebraska grass.

"Even if you can buy tons of hay in Wyoming and Salt Lake, those cattle are still going to be pretty thin by the time you get them to Reno," Ed told her. "You'll need to make sure they've got plenty of water, and it'll take a few weeks in that Washoe Valley to fatten them up again."

"I know. But you've got your own work cut out for you right here handling the rest of the herd and getting the remaining cattle cars in shape for the journey."

"With a week on our hands, we'll build masterpieces."

It was meant as a joke, but Jessie could not smile. She turned to the samurai. "Ed is responsible for the rest of the Circle Star cattle I'm leaving behind. But you, Ki, are responsible for the lives of Miss Linker and the cowboys. Be vigilant."

"Always," he told her.

Ed shouted, "Let's get that car on down the line and get the others loaded!"

Four cowboys roped the loaded cattle car and this time, their horses really had to hump to get momentum. Once moving down the line, however, the fully packed cattle car rolled easily enough. In fact, they had to have men at the depot end to jam logs underneath its wheels to keep it from rolling out onto the main line.

They loaded the remaining cars in a fury of dust and activity, each a minute or two faster than the one previous. And by the time they heard the distant wail of a locomotive steam whistle and saw the speck of the onrushing Union Pacific Railroad, fifteen hundred cattle were ready to freight west.

Both the engineer and the conductor jumped down beside the burned out depot; their faces grim. Jessie, Ed and Ki stepped up to meet the two men. "We're ready to hook up," Jessie said.

"I'm sorry," the conductor said, wagging his head back and forth. "We just can't pull that many cattle cars over the Continental Divide. Don't have the fuel or the steam-power."

"What!" Ed roared.

"You heard him," the engineer said. "Not enough coal. We'd run out of fuel somewhere in Wyoming."

Jessie grew very still inside. "Then I suggest you tell your passengers and crew to disembark and march over to those cottonwoods with axes. You want fuel, cut it right now. But you *are* taking these cattle."

"No, we're not."

Ki stepped in and grabbed the conductor who was in charge of the entire train, then twisted his collar until he was choking. "Say yes ma'am. We will be honored to take your herd to Reno."

The conductor, a big man with a big belly and gruff voice, tried to tear free, but Ki reached up and batted him across the mouth. The blow looked almost like a gentle slap, but it rocked the conductor and broke his lips. "Tell the lady what I asked," Ki said in a soft voice.

The conductor lost his nerve. "All right. All right! We'll cut wood here and take the damn cattle!"

Ki released the man. "We'll even help you."

The order was given. Able passengers and crew piled out of the railroad cars all up and down the line and were ordered into the cottonwood groves along the Platte. Jessie used her supply wagon to help, and within two hours, the train had enough fuel. Then the makeshift cattle cars were coupled to the end of the train.

Jessie stood on the rear platform of the caboose. "You men follow my orders!" she called as the train started to pull away. "If a huge war party comes, you give them the herd and run for Texas!"

Ed nodded and so did the samurai. But in her heart, as that train pulled away, Jessie knew that the Circle Star men would fight to the death before they'd abandon a single Texas steer.

"Miss Starbuck!" the conductor said, about twenty minutes later as the train was steaming at full throttle. "Look there to the south!"

Jessie had just eased down into her first class coach when the man had burst in on her. Now, she glanced across the coach and then rushed to the window on the other side of the car.

Her blood went cold. She saw at least thirty Cheyenne warriors about a mile to the south. Their faces were covered with war paint, and they were galloping east parallel to the line.

Jessie wanted to cry out in helpless fury. The Cheyenne were going to attack her pitifully small crew and slaughter her herd of cattle.

Jessie staggered back to her seat. There was nothing she could do now.

"You got out just in time," the conductor said, "but I sure pity your friends."

Jessie wasn't listening. She was praying.

Chapter 7

Ki watched the Union Pacific train pull away with grave misgivings. He had a highly refined instinct for trouble, and every fiber in his body was tingling with alarm. But at least, Jessie was safe until she reached Nevada.

"I wish she'd have let you go along," Ed Wright said. "Sometimes, that girl just doesn't know the meaning of caution. I never been to the Comstock, but I heard it's a real tail-twister. Jessie had better watch her back close with you stuck out here in Nebraska."

"I'll be at her side in a week," he vowed. "Until then, there's not much I can do but try to help us survive."

Ed shook his head as he watched the westbound train shrink in the huge distance of prairie. "This ain't Texas, but it's still mighty high, wide and lonesome."

"I'm going to be in the saddle most of the time. Now that the cowboys will be spending their days building up the rest of the cattle cars, I should have my pick of the remuda," Ki said.

"Pick a fast one," Ed drawled. "If you run into Indian trouble out there on the plains, there sure ain't no place to hide. All that will save your scalp is a fast horse."

"And my weapons," Ki said. He looked over at Maggie Linker. "Maybe you can help the cook."

"I'd rather work on the cattle cars."

"Hell, let her!" the cook said, obviously taking offense at her honest remark. "She'd just get in my way around here."

"Then that's the way we'll do it," Ed told them. "Miss Linker, you can grab an axe and set off for those felled cottonwood trees down by the river. Trim off the branches so we can split 'em up for flooring."

"Thank you," she said, shooting the cook a grin of triumph and then marching toward the river.

"Independent as hell, ain't she," the Circle Star foreman said with a wink. "I can see you ain't tamed her a lick yet."

"I never intended to 'tame her'," the samurai said as he turned his horse south.

He had already decided that he would make a circle around the burned out Plum Creek Station and pretty much keep moving that way. But just to the west there was a low rise of land that would afford at least some vantage point, and that was where Ki headed.

It was late afternoon, and thunderheads were piling up to the east. When Ki reached the low rise of land, he dismounted. His horse dropped its head and began to graze. Far away, lightning split the still air, and Ki could see that a storm was moving in their direction. It wouldn't bring snow or any real danger, just lightning and some scattered rain before it passed on. The main thing was that Ed and the cowboys saw it coming and bunched the cattle so they wouldn't stampede. At least, Ki thought, with half of them on their way to Reno, the job would be much easier.

He stilled himself and began slowly studying the landscape. When he turned to the west, he saw the small but very distinct figures on horseback moving east along the railroad tracks straight for the Plum Creek Station. Ki stiffened. He wanted to tell himself that the figures were just a distant herd of buffalo, but he knew that was not true. There were no cavalry soldiers in these parts. Even if Jessie sent a message for army help at the next station, it would still be many days before the cavalry arrived, if it arrived at all.

"More Indians," he said, feeling his heart quicken. He grabbed up his reins, swung into his saddle and started back to Plum Creek at a high gallop. He wasn't sure what they could do to save the herd against such a large raiding party. Jessie had taken three cowboys to help her feed the cattle and push them from Reno to Virginia City. That left them pretty short-handed. Too short-handed to fend off a large Indian attack as well as protect the cattle. But one sure thing, they were in for a fight.

Ki's horse was flecked with foamy sweat by the time he reached the burnt-out railroad station. This brought the cowboys running; no man raced a good cowhorse into the ground unless he had a damn good reason.

In as few words as possible, Ki told Ed Wright and the Circle Star cowboys that big trouble was coming their way. "We can make a stand right here or we can try and keep the herd together," he said. "If we choose the latter, some of us are going to die."

Ed made his own opinion known to them all. "Miss Starbuck gave us orders to run, but there ain't a man among you who'd do it. I say we mount up and stampede these cattle right down their throats."

The cowboys answered by racing for their horses. In less than three minutes, they were mounted and galloping off to pull the herd together.

"Here they come!" someone yelled.

The Cheyenne were strung out in a loose battle line. With their bright war paint and feathers, they were a formidable looking bunch. The cowboys began to push the cattle into a trot, then a run as they gathered speed moving toward the Indians.

"Where's Maggie!" Ki yelled, suddenly remembering the girl.

"She's down by the river."

Ki's mount was already played out, but there was no time to change horses or saddles. So he whipped the poor beast down toward the Platte River just as the first scattered rifleshots began.

Maggie must have heard them too because she came running out of the trees with the axe still in her hand. "What . . ."

The words died in her throat when she saw the Indians. The axe fell from her hand, and she ran toward Ki who reached down, plucked her from the grass and swung her up behind his cantle.

When the herd of Texas longhorns and crossbreds struck the line of Indians, several of the Cheyenne were knocked to the prairie and buried under their hooves. Most, however, peeled off to the sides and then came swooping and hollering into the cowboys who were no match for their numbers. Ki could see and hear Ed yelling for his men to abandon the cattle and take cover in the trees along the river. But many a cowpony was already riderless, and Ki knew that they were in danger of being massacred if they did not make an immediate stand.

His own horse was faltering by the time he reached Ed and the surviving Texans who were in full retreat. "The island!" Ki shouted, driving his horse into the Platte until it began to swim.

The arrows all around them were as numerous as hailstones, and two more cowboys died before they reached the river. One of them was the young kid, Pete, who had lost his nerve in the Cimarron River.

The island was their only chance, and Ki prayed that the piles of driftwood would offer enough cover to save them from being overrun. When the cowboys hit the river on their running horses, huge sheets of water exploded into the air. A horse fell, but its rider grabbed the tail of another horse and skidded across the water. A moment later, they were on the island. It was no bigger than a horse corral but provided a good deal of cover.

The Texans threw themselves from their mounts, their Winchesters in one hand, their Colts in the other. They vaulted over the driftwood and took cover in a low, sandy place. Ed was already wounded twice, but neither wound appeared fatal.

"Sonofabitch!" a cowboy shouted, as an arrow buried its point into his shoulder.

Maggie was at his side in an instant. Without hesitation, she tore her shirt and wrapped a strip around the blood-slick haft of the Cheyenne arrow, then yanked it out. The cowboy fainted and Maggie unwound the strip of cloth and jammed it into the bleeding wound. Another arrow nicked her cheek and Ki yelled, "Keep your head down!"

Maggie ducked, but the cowboy next to Ki did not and died. One of the Indians had shot him with an old flintlock rifle. Ki grabbed the cowboy's Winchester and began to shoot. He much preferred his own bow and arrows, but it would have been suicidal to stand up and draw the weapon so he stayed low and kept up a steady fire.

"They're going to try and overrun us!" Ed yelled. "Don't let them cross the water!"

The Texans were doing their damnedest to keep that from happening. But they were down to four fighting men

63

and the Indians seemed countless. And yet, as their Winchesters roared, the Indians took a fearful loss. Brave warriors were being slammed out of their saddles. The shooting was so hurried that neither Ki nor the cowboys bothered to aim for a kill, but instead, just concentrated in unhorsing the warriors until the charge was broken.

The Cheyenne did break. They were brave, but there was not a one of them that wanted to throw his life away foolishly. Since they were being cut to pieces, they had no choice but to throw themselves into the Platte and swim for their lives.

"We did it!" a cowboy shouted.

The gunfire stopped, and the Indians pulled their dead and wounded out of the river and out of rifle range.

"What will they do now?" a Circle Star rider asked.

Ki looked at Ed Wright who shrugged his shoulders and said, "Ki, you've had more experience with Indians than I have, what do you think?"

"I think they've lost more warriors than they'd have believed possible against so few of us. I hope that they'll decide to take what cattle they can round up and head for other parts."

Ed studied his face. "What you hope isn't what will happen though, is it."

"No," Ki said. "They know we're down to four."

"Five," Maggie said.

"All right, five. It's still not much. I think that they'll try to hit us from both sides of the river. Get us in a crossfire tomorrow morning at dawn."

"That ain't what I wanted to hear," Ed told him. "So what do you suggest?"

"I don't suggest anything for the moment," Ki told him and the other bloodied cowboys. "We just have to stick together."

"But what about the cattle?"

"The cattle are lost."

"But . . ."

"Listen," Ki said. "I know you're the cattle boss and you feel responsible for the cattle. But Jessie left me responsible for her men, and we've already been whittled down to a handful. If help arrives, we can go after the cattle then. Until that time, I say we try to hold them off from right here."

"Hell of a place to make a stand," Ed growled.

"It could be a lot worse. We'll dig in and use sand as a barricade," Ki said. "We'll have water aplenty. We can do without food until the next Union Pacific train arrives. Or maybe even the United States Cavalry."

None of them looked pleased with that idea. Ki wasn't too pleased himself. And he really had no intention of just 'diggin in'. What he intended to do was to go after the Cheyenne if they abandoned the siege. And if they stayed in hope of routing out and then killing the last of the Texans, then he'd be paying a visit to their camp every night. He was *ninja*, the invisible assassin. He had been trained to move silent and unseen among the wariest of enemies. He would drive fear into their hearts. Each morning, after each night of feasting on Circle Star beef, they'd awaken to find some of their warriors dead, their horses run off, their weapons broken or rendered useless.

The thing unseen was the thing most feared, by Japanese, by whites, by Indians. Let them wonder how their enemy could steal among them at night, past their guards and their sleepless eyes. Let each of them grow fearful that he would be the next to die. And let them understand the true meaning of *ninja*.

Chapter 8

The train was too long and too heavy for the two engines that struggled to pull it up and over the Wasatch Mountains. The iron monsters labored at full throttle, yet the train had slowed to a walk. It was obvious that they were not going to make it to the summit tunnels.

The passengers were alarmed. Jessie listened to the conductor tell a woman and her husband that everything would be all right. The woman, a matronly looking sort with hard gray eyes and double chins, was not satisfied. "This is outrageous! Mr. Phillips and I paid for safe transportation to Reno."

She looked to her husband, a small, bookwormish fellow for support. The man forced some hollow authority into his voice. "Yes, conductor. I . . . I mean Mrs. Phillips *is* upset. Not only are we at great risk from an Indian attack, but we're also going to be just hours and hours late!"

The conductor threw up his hands in a helpless gesture and said, "I'm afraid we have no choice in this matter. You see, we didn't anticipate hauling all those cattle out of Plum Creek."

"Then get rid of them!" the woman snapped. "The Union Pacific promised we would arrive in Reno at ten o'clock next Friday morning. But we'll be at least a day late. We might even miss Sunday church services, gawdammit!"

Mr. Phillips patted his wife's hand. "Now, Mother. Don't upset yourself so much, it's—"

"Oh, shut up!"

The man cringed in his seat. His adam's apple bobbed up and down as he said, "Conductor, our friends will be worried sick about this delay. Probably figure the entire train had been wiped out by Indians somewhere between here and Omaha."

The conductor expelled a deep breath. "We'll telegraph ahead that we've been delayed. There will be no cause for alarm."

"No cause for alarm!" the woman cried. "Why, if the Cheyenne saw us now, they'd have our scalps. Commit all sorts of unspeakable atrocities against my womanhood."

Jessie almost laughed out loud. Any warrior in his right mind would stay clear of Mrs. Phillips. She looked fit enough to whip a bag of badgers.

She spun around and caught Jessie with a grin she could not conceal. "Did I say something humorous!"

"No, Mrs. Phillips," Jessie answered. "I just wish you would try and relax. I'm sure the engines will pull us over these mountains. And as for the Indians, there are too many armed passengers on board for them to storm the coaches and commit any 'unspeakable atrocities against your womanhood.'"

"Oh?" The woman's eyebrows raised in question. "And what are you, the resident Indian expert?"

Jessie's smile died. She looked out the window and saw that the train had slowed to a creep. She knew that the grade got steeper just before it approached the summit. For the first time, she was concerned that it might actually come to a halt.

"Miss . . . my, Mrs. Phillips asked you a question. Would you please answer?"

"Oh, shut up Arthur!"

Jessie turned to the abrasive woman. "Perhaps you think I ought to unload my cattle and just let this train go on without us."

"Yes! That is a wonderful idea," Mrs. Phillips said. "Precisely the very one I had been considering. Would you be so kind as to tell the conductor that you and those cows will depart so that this train can make it to Reno?"

The conductor drew himself up straight. "I am in charge of the train, Mrs. Phillips. Not you, or Mrs. Starbuck, or the engineer. *I* am in charge. And I've never abandoned any passenger or freight before, and I will not start now."

"Thank you," Jessie said. "But I'm afraid this might be a first."

The conductor peered out the window. He chewed the tip of his silver mustache and said nothing. But it did not take a mind reader to see that he was also beginning to show real concern.

Two miles later, on a high and barren slope of open land that led to the summit tunnels, the train came to a dying halt. Mrs. Phillips, along with all the other passengers were on their feet at once. The conductor tried to calm them down, but it was hopeless. They were still in Indian country and many, many miles from Rock Springs or Salt Lake City, the two nearest towns of any appreciable size.

The conductor jumped down from the landing and strode forward along the railroad bed, and Jessie was right on his heels. She turned to see her cowboys step down from the cattle cars where they were riding. Jessie waved them back to their posts.

"What's wrong!" the conductor yelled up to the engineer.

"Too damned heavy for this grade! We can't build any more steampower or the pressure might blow these boilers apart."

"Damn!" the conductor swore, not realizing that Jessie had followed him.

"Excuse me," Jessie said. "But it seems that my cattle are the problem."

He turned to her. "That's sure the truth, Miss Starbuck. We needed four engines instead of two. Whoever said we could take on fifteen hundred cattle at Plum Creek must have been thinking sheep. Those cattle of yours are too heavy, and we've gotten ourselves into a fix here."

"I know. It seems to me that there's only one solution. We unload the herd and drive them over the summit. How far is it?"

"About twenty more miles of rough country."

"That would mean another six or seven hour delay for you."

"I can't agree to that," the conductor said, shaking his head as if being late was a tragedy not to be endured. We're already behind schedule at least four hours. The Central Pacific locomotives and passenger cars in Ogden have probably already departed. They informed us at Rock Springs that if we didn't make up the time this train would be forced to make the trip all the way to San Francisco. Trouble is, there's another problem. One I'm afraid we can't ignore."

Jessie was a problem solver. She never underestimated difficulties, but neither did she allow herself to dwell on them. The conductor seemed to take the opposite approach and was inclined to be pessimistic. It was a common characteristic, one that Jessie recognized and did tolerate in the managers that she hired to oversee her worldwide corporate interests.

"Go on," she said, curbing her impatience.

The conductor looked down the line of passenger coaches then to the cattle cars at the far end. The train was so long, it stretched around a bend in the track and disappeared so that the caboose was no where in sight. "The trouble is, Mrs. Starbuck, you probably won't be able to drive your cattle through the summit tunnels on top. And the mountainsides are too steep to go around the tunnels. Take a mountain goat to do that."

"Then we really might have a problem," Jessie said, for she had decided only seconds before that they could follow the train. "How long are the tunnels? Can the cattle see light at the far end?"

"No," the conductor said. "The longest is about eight hundred feet, and it curves and blocks the light from either end. Them cattle will never enter that tunnel. It'll seem like a dark old cave. I once tried to drive my pappy's old milk cow into a cave down in—"

"What other choice do we have but to try?" Jessie said, cutting the man off.

"The only thing you can do is drive them back to Rock Springs and wait for the Union Pacific to send enough locomotives to take all your cattle at once."

Jessie was tempted, except there were two problems. The first was that the Union Pacific was not in the business of hauling cattle between Wyoming and Nevada. They didn't have the cattle cars or the locomotives at hand to do such a job. The second was Grant Sawyer and the troubles he faced on the Comstock. Jessie did not want to risk sitting around in Rock Springs for several weeks waiting for a special cattle train to arrive.

"We'll push the cattle up the roadbed in your wake," she

said. "But I've only three cowboys and it won't be easy."

The conductor wasn't pleased. "But what about the tunnels? There's two of them, Miss Starbuck. And the second is the longest. There's just no way you can drive those cattle through."

Jessie shrugged her shoulders. "I don't know if anyone had ever tried to drive a herd through railroad tunnels. We'll just have to face that problem when we get there. Will you wait for us?"

"I just hate to do 'er," the conductor said. "We're already hours late, and you'll never get that herd through. Not even if you had fifty cowboys and horses."

Jessie was getting angry. "Mister, I'll find a way to get the job done. That's a promise. Now, I need your promise that you'll be waiting on the west slope of the Wasatch. If you want to speed things up, then ask some of the passengers to build us a strong cattle chute."

"They won't do that!"

"Well they might if they are asked! Quit being so negative! Maybe all it would take is a half dozen logs to form a bridge from a cut in the roadbed to the opening of a cattle car. Start thinking about what can be done instead of what can't be done."

"That's easy for you to say," the conductor said. "The fact is, you don't have to listen to Mrs. Phillips or some of her kind. There are other important people on this run besides yourself. If they make enough of a stink, I could lose my job. And if I lose my job, there goes my pension, my house, my—"

Jessie was seething. "Mister," she said. "I got a herd of cattle rattling around in some burnt out cars not fit to haul jackrabbits. I got a bunch more cattle back at Plum Creek Station, and a handful of men that are probably fighting the Cheyenne and trying to save their scalps. I have big problems, and they're all because your railroad failed to deliver enough cattle cars or locomotives to do the job they promised. Now, I want your promise that you'll be waiting on the other side of the tunnels when we come through."

"*If* you come through! If, Miss Starbuck. And I know enough about cattle and stock to tell you it can't be done. The only way you could possibly get those cattle through those dark tunnels is if you roped and dragged every single one of them on their backs."

"We'll start unloading," she managed to say. "It'll take a couple hours to build a sturdy loading chute. I suppose you'll be angry because I refuse to just jump my longhorns out the doors and have ten or twenty percent of them break their legs in a pile-up. But I'm not going to do that."

The conductor had heard enough. He turned on his heel and headed back to his coaches. Jessie followed the man and then continued to the cattle cars.

"Something bad wrong?" the first cowboy she came to asked.

"Yes," Jessie said. "We're going to have to unload."

"Right here!"

"That's right."

The cowboy shrugged his shoulders and waved at his companions to come on the run. "It's a bad, bad place to unload," he said, looking at the narrow apron of space between the trackbed and a steep drop-off down the mountainside. It wasn't much better on the up side either.

"We'll build a chute out of logs. Just wedge it into the shoulder and lay it on the lip of the cattle car by the door. Let's move!"

The cowboys exchanged worried glances. They didn't give a damn about anything except Jessica Starbuck and the cattle. And when it came to things going wrong for either of them, they meant to make things right, one way or the other.

The moment the last cattle car was unloaded, the conductor ordered the engineer to start the train moving. Jessie and her three cowboys had more than their share of problems just keeping the spooky cattle all together. A few tried to run up the mountainside, but it was too steep, and they came tumbling down backward. A few others bolted over the down side and went cartwheeling down the slope. Then they dropped over the side of a cliff to fall almost three hundred feet into a river gorge far below.

Most of the cattle attempted to head back for Texas, but Jessie and her cowboys got them turned around and moving up the track toward the tunnel. Once they were lined out and had their minds on the walking, the longhorns and crossbreds reverted to their trail driving instincts and were more manageable. But it was easy to see that, after being cooped up in those cattle cars, they were cranky and just looking for an excuse to raise hell.

"They need water," a cowboy said. "Water and grass."

"They'll have to wait until we get over the top of these mountains and roll down into Ogden," Jessie said. "There's no help for it."

So they drove the cattle on as fast as they would move, which was pretty fast. Because they had been cramped so long, the longhorns were eager and moved with a restless anger.

The country grew more and more spectacular with each mile as they neared the summit tunnels. There were wild gorges and shining silver ribbons of water tumbling down the mountainsides. They saw deer and elk in distant meadows, and up near the higher peaks, they saw a band of bighorn sheep. The pine trees were tall and pungent with pitch; the sky was soft blue, and the clouds were whispy

73

and white. Mountain country, Jessie thought, nice in the spring, summer or fall, but cattle-killing in the winter. She knew something about Wyoming cattle country and this part of Utah didn't look any different. She had many friends in the Wyoming Stock Growers Association head-quartered in Cheyenne and some of them had been wiped out by the hard winters. But soon, they'd be dropping down into what Fremont had called the Great Basin. An eternity of sagebrush and dry hills stretching all the way from the Wasatch to the Sierras.

"I'm going to ride up ahead," she told her cowboys. "The tunnels have to be getting close."

She was right. Less than two miles ahead, she and Sun came to the first tunnel. Jessie tried to ride her palomino through the tunnel, but the animal was unwilling. She spurred the horse, and finally, Sun entered the dark, still smoky cavern. Sun's iron-shod hooves clanged against the steel rails, and he snorted with fear.

"It's all right," Jessie said, urging the fine animal forward and scratching its golden neck with reassurance. "I swear this has an end. I wouldn't send us into a tunnel that dropped off into the middle of the earth."

Sun danced forward, and only a few minutes later, they turned a slight bow in the tunnel and saw the exit with light streaming inside.

Jessie turned Sun around. There was no sense in going all the way through. She knew there would be another tunnel up just ahead. A little longer, but no more or less difficult.

She emerged from the tunnel to see the cattle coming toward her. The moment they saw the dark hole in the mountain, they tried to turn around and come back. Jessie knew they were in for a tough fight.

She rode swiftly around behind the herd and uncoiled

her lariat. She and the Circle Star cowboys drove the bawling cattle toward the mouth of the tunnel. The cattle moved up to the entrance, then would go no further. Heads down the longhorns clicked their horns like castanets against one another, they told Jessie more clearly than words that it was unnatural for them to enter caves. Caves are where mountain lions and bear might be waiting. *No*, they said with their eyes rolling. No!

Both the longhorns and crossbreds steadfastly refused to budge.

"Maybe I could help you," a man said as he walked out of the tunnel and into the sunlight. He planted his boots next to each rail and grinned, looking for all the world like he was the guest of honor at a surprise birthday party. "Howdy, Miss Jessica Starbuck. The honor of this meeting is all mine."

Jessie stared at him. He was tall, broad-shouldered and would have been quite handsome had it not been for a cockiness that bordered on insolence and a scar that ran from his prominent jawline all the way up to the front of his right ear. A saber scar from the looks of it, though it might been inflicted by a bowie knife. What he held in his hand was almost as interesting as his dark, piercing eyes. It was a blacksnake or bullwhip as it was also called. The whip had a short hickory handle about two feet long and a braided leather body that ended with a buckskin popper. The whip was curled up in the man's right hand. It was very long and black.

"Who are you?" Jessie asked.

"The man who is going to deliver these fine Texas cattle to the other side of these mountains. Name is Black Snake Charley, and I'm at your service."

He smiled, removed his Stetson with a flourish and even bowed slightly at the waist. When he straightened, he flashed Jessie a bold look of admiration. "I'll get these cattle through both tunnels for just a dollar a head."

"Mister!" one of the cowboys snarled. "I don't know what snake hole you just crawled out of, but you're crazy!"

Black Snake did not show a hint of anger. He just shrugged his broad shoulders and smiled, then walked over to a place where he was sure not to get stepped on and rolled a cigarette. "If you're that certain of things, then go ahead. I enjoy an amusing show as well as the next man."

The Circle Star cowboy bristled with anger.

"Take it easy, Bob." Jessie frowned. "We aren't getting them through beating them with ropes and we haven't time to lasso and pull every one of them through the tunnel. So I guess I have no choice but to accept Mr. Black Snake's offer."

"But—"

Jessie waved off the protest. "As soon as you finish that cigarette, we'll be pleased to watch *your* show."

Black Snake did finish his cigarette, and by the time he was done, Jessie and her cowboys were as hot as the tip of his smoke.

"How much money am I going to earn?" Black Snake said, grinding his cigarette butt under his heel and uncoiling the long bullwhip.

"There's fifteen hundred head. You'd have to deliver them through both tunnels. Not just this one, which is the shortest."

He chuckled. "To be honest, ma'am, I had thought about getting them stuck in between and then raising my price. You wouldn't have had much choice but to pay, would you."

"Yes I would have. I'd have shot you, then used that whip myself."

His grin melted. "I heard you were as hard as the steel

76

of these railroad tracks and as beautiful as a mountain columbine in the springtime. It's true. But the fact of the matter is, it takes an expert to handle one of these black-snakes. I been practicing for years, just waiting for a chance to hit it big like this."

"Cut the chatter!" a cowboy said. "Let's see you back up your words."

Black Snake circled around behind the herd as he talked. "Cowboy, I can pop a fly out of the air at twenty feet. I can cut a man's smart-alecky lips off before he can say, 'boo!' I can pluck his eyes out too. If I were you, I'd mind my manners."

Something about him made the Circle Star cowboy clamp his lips together.

The stranger shook out his bullwhip and began to move around them. The cattle paid Black Snake no attention. He let his whip trail out behind him, and then his arm suddenly snapped forward in a hard throwing motion.

When the buckskin popper cracked beside the head of the most truculent longhorn in the bunch, it sounded like a .50 caliber buffalo rifle going off right in their ears. The big longhorn bolted forward as if stunned, and when it tried to throw out its front legs and stop, Black Snake's whip caught it right between the legs in one of its most tender parts. The effect was no doubt like being zapped by lightning. The steer actually screeched in a way that none of the Texans had ever heard before. It vaulted with the grace of an antelope right into the train tunnel and took off running; they could all hear it stampeding on through the tunnel.

"That's one dollar," Black Snake said more to himself than to anyone else. "Reckon the rest will come a little easier."

He chose another and his instincts for picking the most

troublesome of the steers was flawless. Again, the bull-whip snapped out, and this time he scorched the steer's backside. The animal spun and thought about charging the horseless punisher. But Black Snake Charley's wicked bullwhip went straight for one of its nostrils and when it popped, the steer almost went to its knees in pain. "Yaaah!" the man screamed as his whip snapped again and again.

The troublesome steer rolled its eyes and all it wanted to do was to get away from the horseless man. It whirled back around toward the tunnel, and with the bullwhip singing the hairs on its behind, it went charging into the dark tunnel.

What happened next, happened so fast that even Jessie was caught by surprise. One minute they were staring at the backside of the second longhorn to go blasting through the tunnel, the very next, the air was exploding like shot and the whip was darting in and out of the herd like the tongue of a rattlesnake. The herd lost its nerve. They started to bolt for the cliff but the man's whip turned them back to the tunnel and drove them forward in a rush. Snorting, farting and bellowing in pain and fear, the herd vanished into the tunnel, and Black Snake Charley disappeared after them.

Jessie and the Circle Star cowboys were speechless for almost a minute. They could hear the whip popping and could almost feel the tunnel tremble.

"Excuse me, ma'am, but I think you just lost fifteen hundred dollars. That wild son of a gun is going to chase them poor cattle right on through both tunnels and not let them stop until they reach Ogden!"

Jessie just shook her head in wonder. "Oh," she said, "I'm pretty sure that Black Snake Charley will not chase them cattle one foot past the west end of the second tunnel.

That was the deal. He does not strike me as a man who would tax himself without it being required. And as for the money, I'll gladly pay him."

The trio of cowboys looked at each other and one said what the others were thinking, "I sure wished I'd have learned to do that!"

Jessie said nothing but just spurred Sun back into the tunnel. She rode through it easier this time because Sun knew that it would not hurt him. She passed through a hundred yards of sunshine and then rode through the second tunnel, which possessed an overpowering mix of smoke and cowshit.

"I'll take my fifteen hundred dollars now," the man said, smoking his cigarette and leaning up against the western portal of the second summit tunnel.

Jessie shook her head. "I don't carry that much cash. I'll pay you as soon as the train arrives in Ogden."

"Damn," Black Snake said. "I was afraid you was going to say that. You see, the cattle cars are waitin' . . . but I'm afraid the rest of the train is long gone."

Jessie's head snapped up and she looked ahead past the rickety cattle cars to see nothing but open space. Her fists clenched, and she shook with fury and tried not to curse out loud in front of a stranger.

"Go ahead and burn my ears," Black Snake said. "Ain't neither one of them still virgins."

"Dammit!" Jessie cried. "The sonofabitch left us!"

"He sure did," the man said. "Now what are you going to do?"

Jessie shook with anger. She did not yet trust herself to answer.

Chapter 9

Jessie stood beside the make-shift cattle cars and weighed her options. The most obvious thing she could do would be to trail her cattle right down the railroad tracks to Ogden, then possibly even turn them south down to Salt Lake City. There was no doubt in her mind that she might be able to sell the cattle in Utah, but there would be little if any profit. The Mormons were fine people, great farmers and ranchers who also happened to be very clannish and tight-fisted. They strongly preferred to deal with each other, and Jessie had no doubt that her cattle would not bring a good market price. At least, not half what they'd bring in Reno.

But getting the herd to Reno posed a big, big problem because the train would only delay for a few hours in Ogden and then would rush on across the deserts. It was already behind schedule, and she had no doubt that the conductor who had betrayed and abandoned her would want to put as much distance between them and his train as was humanly possible.

"I don't see any help but to trail them on down to the flatlands and then wait for next week's train," she said, making it clear that the choice of waiting in the Mormon state of Desert for another train was not to her liking.

"There is still a way to get these cattle to Reno...
maybe even by Friday," Black Snake said.

"The hell there is!" a Texan said in frustration. "The
train is gone. It'll take us 'til Friday just to get these cattle
off this mountain and down to Salt Lake City."

"Not if you loaded 'em back into those old cattle cars
and each of us stood on the hand brake."

"What!" Jessie cried.

"It'd work," Black Snake said. "Sure, the Indians burnt
off the sides and flooring, but not the brakes or the brake
handles or any of the rest of the brake parts. Take a look if
you don't believe me. It's still all there 'cause it's all
metal. Won't burn. Can't burn."

Jessie took a peek under the new flooring of each cattle
car. Sure enough, Black Snake was right. "It does seem to
be intact."

"'Course it is," the man said. "You could load these
cattle cars and we could run these Texas longhorns down to
the basin quick as you please."

"But what good would that do me?" Jessie asked. "By
the time we got to Ogden, even assuming we could coast
all the way, by that time, the train would be moving on to
Reno."

"I don't think so," Black Snake said matter-of-factly.

"Miss Starbuck," Bob growled, "I think we've all had
about enough of this smart-alecky son of a gun so if you
don't mind, I'll—"

Black Snake's hand shot out, and the wooden handle of
his whip struck the Texas cowboy under the jaw and
knocked him on his back. "I guess you had better start
learning to speak more mannerly," he said.

Bob was a fighter, a man in his early twenties, hot-
headed but not vicious. Jessie almost ordered him not to
fight, but she knew that Bob would seethe until anger poi-

soned him and became hatred. So she let her cowboy jump to his feet and wade into the tall stranger.

It wasn't much of a contest. Black Snake Charley's hands were so fast they blurred the vision. He ducked a looping overhand and then planted a booming uppercut into Bob's solar plexis. The Texan was lifted clear off the ground, and his cheeks puffed out like those of a croaking bullfrog. When he landed back on his feet, he was sucking for air, and Black Snake drove a straight left into his jaw that sent him backpedaling into the dark tunnel. They all heard him hit the tunnel floor and groan.

The other two cowboys jumped from their horses and were ready to take their licks as well, but now Jessie stepped in between and said, "That's enough! The next man that throws a punch can ride—or walk—on out of here. I won't have anymore squabbling among ourselves. Things are difficult enough."

The pair of Texan cowboys were quick to back off. It was damned hard to get on the Circle Star payroll. It often took years to get a recommendation, and once a man became that ranch's employee, he had a top-paying job for as long as he wanted. If he got stomped by a bronc or gored by a longhorn, Jessie Starbuck would take care of him no matter how long it took. When he got too old to ride the fence lines or roundups, he'd earn his keep working around the ranch headquarters. Being a Circle Star cowboy was something that counted down in Texas. It counted for loyalty and it counted for pride. The pair of cowboys decided Black Snake Charley was not worth losing their jobs for. Besides, after seeing what he had done with Bob, without even using his bullwhip, they weren't too sure they'd have had much of a chance against him even two on one.

"Mr. Black Snake," Jessie said, "a few minutes ago you intimated that we could catch that train to Reno. Now, I've seen the schedule and I know that they won't be in Ogden long enough to overtake them before they depart."

"Well, now," the man said. "For . . . oh . . . say, another five hundred dollars, I'll tell you exactly how you can catch that train."

The two cowboys were furious. One of them said, "You bleedin' bloodsucker!"

But Jessie raised her hand. "If you can tell me how to catch that train, I'll get the extra five hundred from the railroad for abandoning my herd. So let's hear your idea."

The man grinned. "I sure hope you're as honorable as you are pretty, Miss Starbuck. The way I figure it, you're gonna owe me two thousand dollars in Ogden."

Jessie said nothing but just stared at the man as if he were a curiosity. She had never seen anyone with such brass. But so far, he'd backed up his talk with results. They had gotten through the summit tunnels, and they'd never have done it without him.

"Well," Black Snake began. "First off, we load these cattle and coast on down to the Ogden. Now, there are some risks. Cattle cars are heavy and brakes have been known to burn away and fail. But I'll volunteer to take the lead car. I've worked as a brakeman once. I can show the others how it's to be done."

"What about the cars without enough men to handle the brakes?"

"That's not such a problem. See," he said, climbing up on the ladder of the cattle car and grabbing the brake wheel. You set the brake so it rolls but not too fast. You set it just right, then each of us takes every other car and makes adjustments as we go along."

"Sounds dangerous as anything," Jessie said.

"Well, I also heard you were a dangerous woman!" the man said with a wink of his eye. "That you steal the heart of every man that ever sees you, and you never give 'em so much as a smile. Now, that's pretty dangerous."

Jessie could not help but smile. The man was incorrigible but he was also one of a kind. "There now, I've given you my smile, now tell me why the train will be waiting—assuming we don't all wreck on the way down this mountainside."

"Well," Black Snake said. "The truth of the matter is, I overheard that conductor when he promised you he'd wait until you got through these tunnels. And when he didn't, I got so darned mad I jumped off the train and shot three holes in both of the locomotive's boilers."

"What!"

"I know. It was a shameful thing to do. Wasn't easy, either. But I knew where the thinnest metal was and I did borrow an old Spencer repeating rifle. It had enough whallop to punch the holes, and when that train pulled away, why, I could see the engineer was fit to be tied. He was *real* mad."

Jessie was aghast. She could not believe her ears. "You shot holes in the locomotive boilers?"

"Yep. I figure they'll make Ogden 'cause it's all downhill, but not as fast as they'd planned. And they'll have to hold up for delays. I worked on them boilers once. You can patch 'em good as new. But it takes some time and some doin'. Yep. There ain't much doubt in my mind that it'll take five or six hours. Ought to be enough for us to get there—if we start loading right now."

Jessie studied the man's strong face. It was good face, even with the scar. There was something a little dangerous about Black Snake Charley, but also very mysterious and intriguing. He had a strong sense of honesty—not of fair play—but of honesty. Jessie liked that.

"All right," she said. "Let's see you help us earn another five hundred dollars."

"At your service, ma'am. As soon as your cowboys drag us that loading chute, I'll drive the cattle aboard faster'n you could believe possible."

Once they revived Bob, Jessie and her cowboys set right to work. They rode back through the tunnels to where the loading chute lay. They roped it and dragged it through the tunnels to the empty cattle cars and then dismounted and lifted it up to the doorway. After that, they let Black Snake sort and drive the cattle back up into the cattle cars. After going through a train tunnel, it did not seem to bother them at all.

They had the cattle all loaded and the hand brakes set within two hours. True to his word, Black Snake took the first car, and with the cattle bawling and his brake starting to screech, he raised his arm and made a half-turn motion that left no doubt as to what the Texans should do.

Jessie was second in line. The hand-brake was stiff and rusty but it turned if you put your body into the effort. She felt her cattle car and the one pushing along behind it begin to move and her feelings were a mixture of elation and fear.

"Yeee-haww!" Black Snake yelled, tearing off his Stetson and hurling it into the wind.

Jessie turned the brake a little freer and the cattle car picked up speed. The mountain air began to whip her reddish-blonde hair around, and down below, the longhorns bawled anxiously. Jessie was clinging to the front of the cattle car at least fifteen feet off the ground. The only solid thing she had was the hand brake and the iron ladder leading up to what had once been the roof of the car.

Behind her, she saw the other cowboys also letting up on the brakes, and like a long, segmented worm, the cattle

85

cars began to roll faster and faster. This was absolutely insane! She gripped the iron brake wheel, and every instinct told her to crank it down and bring this madness to an end. But then she looked up at Black Snake Charley, and even though his cars had pulled ahead almost three hundred yards, she could still see the grin on his face.

Jessie did not apply the brakes. Instead, she eased up on them and her cattle cars began to roll faster and faster as they gained on those ahead of her. Black Snake Charley saw her closing the gap and he worked his brake so his cars ran faster.

Damn him! Jessie thought, isn't he a piece of work, though!

So they started their race, a race down thirty-five miles of mountainside. Sometimes the cattle cars got to rolling so fast that it seemed that they would shake all apart. The longhorns, brave as grizzlys in their own natural surroundings, were terrified but their bawling could not be heard over the banging of the track. Now and then a cottonwood pole would break loose and go hurtling off like a giant spear. Many times Jessie would see Black Snake Charley frantically working to slow his cattle cars and know that there was a sharp bend coming up. So she'd frantically duplicate his efforts, sometimes just enough to keep her cattle car from breaking free of the rails and flying into space.

The race seemed to last for hours, and Jessie's heart had never beat faster as the cattle cars streaked across massive trestles spanning gorges and whipped around mountainsides almost on one set of outside wheels. But finally—all good things must come to an end—she saw the Great Basin and far, far down a gentle grade, the dim outline of Ogden, Utah Territory.

Like the man before her, Jessie released the brakes and

let the cars race down to the settlement. As she drew closer, she saw that, just as Black Snake had promised, the locomotive was still undergoing boiler repairs. Black Snake brought his lead cattle cars right up to the rear of the passenger train and they'd crash together and be coupled.

Jessie was out another pile of money, but she did not care a whit. The ride down off the Wasatch was worth ten thousand dollars any old day. And when she tracked down the conductor and gave him a little hell, that would be worth even more.

Jessie stood beside the coach and counted out the money to Black Snake. When he had it all, he smiled and said, "You want it back?"

She blinked. "What do you mean?"

"Well, I know you're a mighty rich woman, but this is a lot of money. I'd trade it for a couple of days alone with you, Miss Starbuck."

The corners of Jessie's mouth curved in a smile. This man was impossible, yet she could not help but feel flattered. "You told me you'd been waiting all your life for a chance to make this kind of money."

"Oh, I have! But I'll spent the rest of my life wondering what it would have been like being close to you. Curiosity unsatisfied is a terrible thing, Miss Starbuck."

"I'm sure it is," she said. "But there are worse things. Keep your money, Black Snake Charley. It's the wrong time and the wrong place. One of my oldest and dearest friends was murdered on the Comstock. I can't wait a second longer to find her murderer."

"Is that the only reason?"

"No," she admitted. "Another reason is that I don't go to bed for money. I don't need it."

He chuckled. "Well now, that does put you in a class all by yourself, doesn't it."

She had no answer for that.

He grabbed her before she could turn and walk away. His arms were long and strong, and he pulled her up hard against his lean body and kissed her hungrily. "Maybe some day we'll meet again. A better time and a better place," he said.

Jessie pulled away. "I doubt it. But thanks . . . for the cattle and the wild train ride."

"What about the kiss?"

She laughed. "You got as good as you gave! You don't deserve any thanks for that."

Jessie turned away from the man and stepped onto the train. She did not know why he was staying in Ogden, and it was not her business to ask. All she knew was that he was an enigma. A mystery that would probably never be solved by anyone. He was unpredictable, wild, dangerous and cocksure of himself. He was the kind of man that, even with that saber scar, would break a woman's heart in every town. He was, in short, bad medicine.

She waved to him as the train pulled out of the Ogden station—with her cattle—and headed for Reno.

Chapter 10

Ki knew they needed food. Just after sunset, the Cheyenne had slaughtered several Circle Star steers and built several campfires about a hundred yards beyond rifle range. After leaving several guards to make sure the Texans did not attempt to escape from the river island, the rest of the warriors began preparing the feast. Even now, the Texans could smell their own beef cooking.

"Dammit, if this isn't the last straw!" Ed Wright said. "Here we are sworn to protect Circle Star cattle, and all we can do is hug this sand pit and slaver all over ourselves as our own beef gets barbecued! I tell you, it's enough to make a cowboy do something crazy."

"That's exactly what they're hoping for," Ki said. "They know we probably lost or ruined our provisions in the river. They figure to starve us out over the next few days. Make us run."

"Run on what! We had to let our horses go or they'd have looked like pincushions!"

"Run on our feet," the samurai said, then added with his dry sense of humor, "but they don't know that a Texas cowboy would rather face a hundred Indians than suffer the indignity of walking any distance."

The cowboys forced a grin, which was quite an effort considering their miserable circumstances.

What else can we do but run?" Maggie asked.

"I intend to go into their camp and get us some of that beef," Ki said.

"What!"

"Let's have our own barbecue. I believe that would give the Indians something to consider."

Maggie pressed close to him. "You can't do that. You'll be killed for sure. Why, they've warriors posted right there on the shore to watch us."

Ki wanted to assure her, though he knew that the risks were considerable. The Indian was a very worthy opponent, one who would test a samurai's skills. "They watch, but that doesn't mean they must see all," Ki said, slipping into his *ninja* costume and pulling the hood over his head so that only his eyes showed.

"So," Ed declared. "Now we get to see a real samurai in action. A *ninja*."

While the Circle Star foreman explained what little he knew of *ninjutsu*, "the art of the invisible assassin," Ki mentally prepared himself for the task that lay ahead. He fell into a deep state of concentration and dimly he heard Maggie trying to speak to him. But he focused on his mind and body control until there were no sounds or distractions while he reviewed his weapons and skills, then visualized himself fighting the Cheyenne enemies.

He had *shuriken* blades and his *tanto* knife with its long, thin blade encased in a lacquered wooden sheath. He also had a *han-kei*, a half-sized version of the *nunchaku*, two short pieces of wood joined by a few inches of braided horsehair. The *nunchaku* fit together perfectly flush so that Ki could use them with great pressure, like the closing jaws of a tiger. A finger, wrist, or other joint caught between the sticks would crack like a pecan shell in a nutcracker. He could perform virtually every *te* block and strike, yet wanted the extra power and the centrifugal force generated when he whipped one of the *nan-kei* handles around and around on the end of their horsehair braid. The *han-kei* had many other uses. Flail-like blows could shatter a blocking forearm, and thrusts could easily smash the face or throat of an onrushing enemy. And though Ki did not often use the *han-kei*, it was one of his favorite weapons.

Ki waited a few moments, then roused himself from his deep concentration. Maggie's face reflected such a concern that Ki attempted to ease her worry. "I *will* return," he promised.

"How can you be so sure?"

"I am because I am," he said. "I can be killed, but not this way. It's . . . it's just something that I know. My destiny is not to die here on the prairie, but to serve Jessica Starbuck well and for many more years."

"I don't understand that," she told him. "And I don't even care about your samurai loyalty to another woman. All I want is to know you will not die out there."

Ed Wright's voice was a growl but it was all show and everyone knew it. "Miss Linker, I'll tell you this much, the samurai has more lives than a goddamn cat. But unless he remembers to come back here with some roasted beef, he'll be facing four hungry Texas cowboys that will give him more grief than he ever thought possible!"

Everyone chuckled at that, and Ki was grateful because it broke the tension. Even Maggie seemed to relax a little. "How long will you be gone?"

"No more than an hour," Ki told her.

She started to say something but he turned and left her because there really was nothing left to say. He was *ninja*, and they could not fully understand how he had dedicated thousands of hours to the art of stealth, silence in movement, and swift—if need be lethal—attack.

Ki slid out of the sand-pit and moved across the sand in plain view as he made his way to the Platte River. He was not observed because he had delayed his departure until the Indian guards were distracted by other warriors bringing them smoking Circle Star beef right off the fire. The guards were so hungry, they paid attention to nothing but their meat. Ki slipped into the river. As he swam he created a faint ripple in the water, smaller than that made by numerous muskrats that lived along the riverbank. The samurai allowed the current to carry him downriver about eighty yards. Then he slipped up onto the bank and waited while the water drained from his clothes. Once again, as he felt the *shuriken* blades, his *tanto* blade and the deadly *han-kei*, he was reminded that a samurai was not dependent upon black powder for his own protection. Had he needed a gun, it would have been impossible to keep it dry and in working order while crossing the river.

The Indian encampment consisted of three campfires around which the Cheyenne were gathered. Relying upon their guards, they were enjoying their good fortune of capturing an entire herd of Texas cattle. And while there were still a few isolated herds of buffalo to hunt, they had grown fond of beef and were anticipating the taking of even more white scalps.

Their war chief, a man named Crow Feather, was a lean, hawk-faced warrior who had been on many raiding parties and had fought many battles. He hated the whites and had vowed to his warriors that they would stay until those barricaded on the island were dead. During his own thirty years of life, he had seen the whites invade the Plains, slaughter the buffalo, and send a ribbon of steel across the Indian lands. Soldiers had come and they had built fortresses that were strong and defensible. Crow Feather's own brother and father had been killed by white soldiers. Fifty years ago, there were no soldiers, only their enemies, the Crow, the Ute and the Sioux. Now, the Indians had come together in hope of driving the white men off the Plains. In these days, Sioux and Cheyenne, Crow, Pawnee and Blackfeet were brothers at war.

The chief left his warriors and strode down to the bank of the river. He knew that he was within range of the rifles, but he also knew that he was not afraid. The Great Spirit would call him from his warriors whenever he wanted, there was no need for fear. A war chief was expected to die in battle. In fact, it was his lot to stake himself to the earth in the middle of a fight and, by this act, show that he expected to either live in victory, or die in defeat, but never to run. This, Crow Feather had done many times. The chief studied the dark silhouettes on the island. He wondered if it might not be better to simply charge the whites at dawn and overrun them. But he knew his first responsibility was to take care of his warriors. There were so many whites coming onto the Plains that every warrior who died must give his own life only after taking many scalps.

Crow Feather had already lost almost a dozen warriors trying to reach the entrenched whites, and he was unwilling to lose more to the white men's bullets while his men tried to ford the strong current. So they would wait, and when the whites were weak from hunger and fear, *then* they would attack. The idea of leaving the whites and simply driving their cattle off never occurred to the Cheyenne war chief. The beef would keep his people alive all through another year. But the whites must be destroyed, even tortured if possible for they had killed many good warriors. If the woman could be spared, then he would claim her for

Crow Feather, for he had seen her face, and she was fair to the eye and very brave.

Sixty yards away, the samurai watched as Crow Feather stood beside the water within rifle range, in open defiance of the Texans. Ki suspected that they would have already put a bullet through the chief if Ed had not been afraid of hurting Ki's chances of infiltrating the camp and demoralizing the Cheyenne.

The samurai decided to stampede both the cattle and the horse herd right through the Indian camp. In the resulting noise and confusion, he would slip among the Indians and have his way with as many as possible. And before he left, he would try and steal the roasting beef.

There were two guards watching the large herd of Indian ponies while the rest of the war party ate and celebrated. They were the youngest, most inexperienced of the warriors and though no danger was anticipated they were expected to be alert.

But they were not alert. They sat together, legs crossed and talked. Before being sent out to guard the herd, they had managed to get some uncooked beef and were now eating it with their hands. In the moonlight, the samurai moved closer and closer to the unsuspecting pair. He slipped the polished wooden *han-kei* from his pocket. When he was within ten yards, he dropped down into a crouch, and then like a cougar rushing an unsuspecting doe, he swiftly rushed to the attack.

The Cheyenne youths did not see him until he was almost on top of them, and by then it was far too late. Ki delivered a sweep kick to the first Indian's face. The Cheyenne guard was unconscious before he hit the grass. The second guard had an extra moment to shout a warning to the Indian camp but he failed to do so. Instead, he decided to reach for his knife. He was slender and cat-quick, and Ki admired his courage if not his judgement. When the warrior's knife came forward, Ki used his *han-kei* with devastating effect. Down came the wooden handle, and had he wished, he could have shattered the Indian's forearm, but instead he struck the knife blade and it went spinning. The Cheyenne jumped at the samurai but was stopped in his tracks by a savage flat-foot kick to the midsection. He grunted and collapsed. Writhing on the ground, the Indian finally made a desperate attempt to call for help. Ki dropped to one knee, and his hand found the Cheyenne's neck. His powerful fingers sank down on an *atemi* or pressure point. At once, the Indian youth ceased to struggle.

Ki came swiftly to his feet. He studied the camp and once satisfied that no one was alerted to his actions, walked into the horse herd. The animals studied him warily for they had never seen a man as *ninja*. He spoke to them in a quiet manner, and when he found a long-legged buckskin that seemed unafraid, Ki reached out with his hand. The horse regarded him with interest. Ki rubbed its muzzle, and then his left hand slipped into his *ninja* outfit and produced a thin but very strong bowstring, an extra he carried. While speaking to the animal, he fashioned a crude halter. Before the buckskin quite realized it, the halter was applied, and the samurai was swinging onto his back.

Once again, Ki glanced back toward the Indian camp. Satisfied that the Cheyenne had not yet been alerted to his presence, he began to circle the horses and slowly drive them toward the herd of Circle Star cattle who were plenty wide awake and already starting to climb to their feet.

Suddenly, an Indian cried out a warning, and Ki knew that he had been seen against the backdrop of moonlit sky. The samurai pounded his heels into the buckskin's ribs, and the animal shot forward. Ki circled the herd of cattle and Indian ponies and turned them toward the Cheyenne camp. For a moment, he almost felt sorry for the scattering Indians.

The Cheyenne were caught flat-footed before the stampede. They grabbed their weapons and ran for their lives or else raced for the Platte River knowing that the cattle and horse would turn at the riverbank.

Crow Feather grabbed his hunting bow and quiver. He meant to stand his ground until the last possible instance because he wanted to see and remember the man who now dared to humiliate him and his warriors. Perhaps, he reasoned, he might even manage to fire one deadly arrow and reclaim his own honor. Crow Feather drew back his bow and felt the earth shiver under his feet as the herd came towards him. Now! Now he saw the—

The war chief's blood chilled, and the drawn arrow dropped forgotten from his bowstring. The Cheyenne took a backstep, and a cry of disbelief rose in his throat. He did not fear the onrushing herd of wild-eyed cattle. He did not fear death from earthly things, but what he saw looming closer on the back of a horse could not be earthly. It was headless, faceless and terrible. It was, Crow Feather thought, an evil spirit that had come up from the center of the world to kill the Cheyenne.

Crow Feather began to backpedal toward the river. He could not take his eyes off the thing on the horse. He tipped his head back and cried out for his own spirits to protect him. And at the very instant the first longhorn steer hooked him through the chest and slung him under the hooves of the herd, Crow Feather had tried to turn and flee.

Ki saw the war chief go down under the leaders of the herd. He knew that the Cheyenne would have another chief to replace him before the night was over. Ki heard rifle fire and saw the herd of cattle and Indian ponies come to the edge of the river and then dig their heels into the riverbank and stop. For two, perhaps three minutes, all would be confusion. Then the Cheyenne would regroup. The Indians were not inexperienced in warfare, and they would quickly realize that there was at least one enemy among them and possibly more. As soon as they spotted Ki on horseback, they would come after him.

Ki dismounted and ran over to the campfires. The stampede had left nothing of value in its wake so he ran to the only campfire that had not been in the direct path of the onrushing horses and cattle.

There was a side of beef still roasting on the campfire. Ki yanked the bubbling smoking beef off the fire. He knew it would burn his hands and body if he tried to pick it up and run. So, with great regret, he tore off his ninja costume and threw it over the side of roasting beef, then rolled it up and hoisted it in both arms. It weighted a good hundred pounds, and he could feel its heat and imagine the joy such a bounty would bring to Ed, Maggie and the Circle Star cowboys pinned down and starving in the middle of the Platte.

A pair of Cheyenne warriors saw him in his nakedness, and there was no doubt in their minds that he was man, not an evil spirit. They shouted in anger and rushed him.

With a hundred pounds of burning beef in his arms, the samurai was faced with a hard choice. He did not want to fight anymore, but neither was he willing to abandon the beef and run for his life. So Ki did the only thing he could do—turn and face his enemies. He saw one draw his bowstring and release an arrow from only a few yards away. Ki braced himself, and when the arrow bit into the side of beef, he dropped it and charged with the two-handled *han-kei* twirling overhead. The warrior with the bow tried to grab his knife, but Ki brought one of the wooden handles down hard, and this time, he did shatter his opponent's wrist. The warrior shouted in pain even as Ki swung around and drove his foot into the second man's knee, twisting him into the dirt. Ki was on him in an instant, and he brought the rock-hard edge of his hand down across the base of the fallen warrior's neck, and the Cheyenne would fight no more this night. The Indian with the shattered wrist tried to pick up his knife with his good hand, and Ki used a sweep-kick to drive him over backward.

Picking up the side of beef, the samurai raced for the water. He could see flashes of gunfire coming from the island and decided to stay clear until the shooting died down. In an hour or two, he could rejoin Maggie and the Circle Star crew. Until then, he would hide along the riverbank and enjoy a hot meal.

It was sometime after midnight before he reached the island with his precious cargo. Maggie threw her arms around his neck and hugged him while Ed and the famished cowboys gobbled down the beef.

"How is it?" Ki asked.

"A little gritty," a cowboy said, "what'd ya do, Samurai, drag it across the sand?"

"Aw shut up," Ed groused. "My only complaint was that it's still half alive. Why didn't you wait until it was cooked a little longer?"

Ki smiled. They were teasing him. He liked that. Like the fact that, no matter how bad a fix this seemed, they still had a sense of humor.

They'd need it. As Ki held the woman and studied the distant Indian camp, he could see that the Cheyenne were mighty upset. Maybe upset enough to attack at daybreak. But if they did, then they did. At least the cowboys wouldn't be griping about how they were going to die hungry.

"Eat," Ki told the woman.

"I'd rather hold you." There was a familiar huskiness in her voice that he understood. After the fear she had known for his safety, she wanted to make love to him in celebration of his return.

Ki smiled. "Eat first, then maybe we can figure something out."

Maggie kissed his mouth and went to eat. Ki wondered how much the woman would enjoy making love in the river.

At dawn, the Cheyenne did attack but without spirit or real intensity. Four Indians died, and the charge was broken before things got too serious. Then, the Cheyenne retreated back to the riverbank and remade their camp.

"What the hell are they gonna do!" Ed growled.

"They're going to wait us out," Ki said. "They're going to stay right where they are until we eat all this beef or go crazy and try to escape."

"Then they'll wait until hell freezes over!"

Ki nodded. "Or until either the army or the next train comes along."

Chapter 11

On Friday evening, just as dusk was creeping across the land and the Sierra Nevada Mountains were beginning to glow in the sunset, the train finally pulled into Reno. It was nine hours late and as Jessie hurried toward the cattle cars, she could hear her cattle bawling with hunger and thirst. Still underpowered but no longer forced to assault any mountains, the train had crawled and dragged its long line of cars across Nevada and Utah Territory. Under the best of circumstances, shipping this many cattle would have been difficult but she had done so under the absolute worst of circumstances. Jessie considered it a testimony to the Texas cattle that they could remain standing after so many hours of hunger and thirst.

Now, as she and her cowboys quickly unloaded the herd, she was shocked to see that the cattle resembled walking skeletons. "Let's drive them along the Truckee River toward the mountains," she called to her men as she saddled and bridled her horse, then rode it down the loading chute.

The Texans were as eager as their cattle to see grass and water. Nothing hurt a good cowboy quite as much as watching their stock suffer. And since the cowboys had ridden with the cattle, they'd seen the worst of it. In twenty minutes, they had every Circle Star cow out and moving west toward the Truckee.

"Hey!" a man yelled, galloping after the herd. "Miss Starbuck, you owe the Union and Central Pacific about eighteen hundred dollars shipping fees."

Jessie swung around to see a fat man with a red face. He had a huge belly and a sheet of invoices in his fist. "Mister," she said, "you can contact my lawyers in San Francisco or in Houston, Texas. Your company not only failed to meet its promised commitment for cattle cars and enough locomotives to get this herd to Reno, but your conductor betrayed me in the Wasatch Mountains. He pulled out and left us at the summit tunnels."

The stockyard foreman drew his horse up. "Miss Starbuck. Now, I know you're a rich woman, and I also know that eighteen hundred dollars ain't a whole hell of a lot of money to you. And finally, I can get you in touch with the best cattle buyers in Reno and despite the looks of these cattle, I'll by-God guarantee you the top Nevada dollar. Maybe enough to offset this shipping bill."

Jessie was in no mood for conversation. "Mister, I'm not going to tell you again," she said. "I'm not paying the railroad one thin dime. And as for your cattle buyers, well, I don't need them. After I fatten and rest this herd, I intend to sell these cattle directly to the miners on the Comstock Lode. And I'll make a profit."

"*Then* will you pay this bill?" The fat man had run out of bluster.

"I'll pay that bill when hell freezes over," she said, using Ed Wright's favorite expression. "I'm not here because of your railroad, but in spite of it."

"I never seen anyone so stubborn as you," the man said, taking his hat off and scratching his bald head. "And I never seen cattlecars like the ones you fixed up to haul these poor cattle."

"They did the job," she said, continuing along after her herd and making the stockyard man trot along behind her.

"Well, then, just how much you want for those big-horned rascals!"

"Seventy dollars."

"A head!"

Jessie hid a smile. "That's right."

"You're crazy, Miss Starbuck. Why, those cattle won't bring a cent more than thirty dollars a head in Reno. You maybe get ten dollars more on the Comstock, but not much."

Jessie breathed a deep sigh of relief. She'd been offered sixteen dollars a head in Abilene and she'd paid old Jake twenty-one dollars. It had been her intention to double her money on a trip she'd have had to make anyway and now, she'd bluffed this man and learned some mighty good news. If he said she could get forty dollars on the Comstock, that meant she could get fifty or sixty. And even if she did decide to pay the railroads something for their fare, she'd still come out far ahead of what she'd have gotten in Abilene. There were some who'd say that it was not worth the effort to bring a herd all the way to Nevada, but Jessie would disagree. If Ki and her other cowboys were all right, then it had been a gamble that had paid off handsomely.

"I can offer you thirty-three dollars a head right here and now," the stockyard foreman was saying. "As skinny as they are with them ribs showing, I can still go that high, Miss Starbuck."

Jessie shot the man a cold smile. "Mister, you know exactly where you can go."

The man jerked his horse up to a standstill. "You may be rich," he yelled as she galloped after herd. "But you're in Nevada, not Texas. In this country, you don't have any strings to pull. You better think twice about that herd."

Jessie's smile died on her lips. She was being threatened and threats always made her furious. If Ki had been here, she'd have allowed him to set the man straight about the wisdom of trying to intimidate Jessica Starbuck. In fact, if she had not been so concerned about the welfare of her cattle, she'd have straightened the man out herself!

The cattle rushed to the Truckee, and she let them drink their fill. The sun had already dipped into the Sierra mountaintops and because this was high-desert country, the temperature had cooled very fast.

"We'll push them right over there against that low hill where the grass looks good and nutritious," she said to her weary cowboys. "Then we'll make camp and let them spend a week or two here before we push them south to the Comstock."

The cowboys nodded. They quickly gathered wood and made a campfire, but they'd all forgotten about anything to eat for themselves.

"Miss Starbuck?"

"Yeah."

"What about them Cheyenne Indians we saw riding east, following the train tracks toward Plum Creek?"

"I don't know," Jessie said. "I told them, if there was trouble, just to leave the herd and head for safety."

"But ya know they wouldn't have."

Jessie stared into the fire and pulled the collar of her coat closer around her neck. "Yes," she said quietly, "I know. But our boys are fighters. Ki will see the Indians before they get too close so there is no danger that they'll be caught by surprise. The rest of it is out of our hands. They have their job to do, we've got ours."

The men nodded. "That Black Snake fella, you ever meet anyone like him, Miss Starbuck."

"Never," she said, meaning it.

"I think he was about half crazy, that's what I think."

"Like a fox," Jessie said. She leaned back on the fleece lining of her saddle and pulled her saddle blankets over her for warmth. Tipping her Stetson over her eyes, she said, "Goodnight. Joe, you take the first watch of three hours. Wake me at midnight for the second. Bob, you, then Slim to daybreak."

"Yes, ma'am," Joe said, rising to his feet and heading for his horse. "These tall mountains hanging right over our heads make me nervous. I'll be glad to get back to Texas some day."

Jessie agreed. She felt her stomach rumble with hunger. First thing in the morning, she was going back into Reno, buy a buckboard and stock it with plenty of supplies for her men. They'd suffered, and she was going to make sure they ate well the rest of the time they were away from the ranch. And after she had them settled, she was heading for the Comstock Lode.

The thought of Sarah Sawyer's death took all the satisfaction out of making a profit on her cattle. Jessie had been on the Comstock a time or two. It was rough and ready living. Brutal and unforgiving. She just hoped that Grant Sawyer wasn't already dead.

In the morning, she went into town and bought provisions for her men. They had brought their bedrolls, but the cook had kept the cooking and eating utensils so she purchased a frying pan, a coffee pot and some other odds and ends. She even bought her men a bottle of whiskey to share because they were too short-handed to go into Reno, and it had been a long time since they'd had a drink . . . or a woman.

And all three needed to be with women. Though they would never let on their desires, sometimes Jessie caught one or the other of them staring at her as longingly as if she were a delicious meal.

Jessie could not fault her young cowboys for that. They were men and had not had an opportunity to be with a woman since leaving Texas. As soon as she fattened and sold the herd, she would pay them their wages and turn them loose on Virginia City. There were plenty of saloons and plenty of women eager to satisfy their itch.

It was almost noon before she had delivered the supplies and was ready to leave for the Comstock. "Joe, you're in charge. I want you to graze the herd up toward the mountains and then turn them south. There's a big valley just north of Carson City. I'll come down from Virginia City and meet you there in two, maybe three weeks. Watch out for thieves and don't cross anyone's land without permission."

She gave the Circle Star cowboy five hundred dollars. "This is to be used only in case of trouble. If you should happen to cross a farmer's land, or if the best grass is claimed, use that money to buy grazing rights. I expect these cattle to put on at least two hundred pounds between now and then."

Joe nodded. "By the way they're eatin', I'd guess they will, Miss Starbuck."

Jessie looked to the other men. "This part of the country is beef-starved and you may have some trouble. No doubt, you'll have buyers coming around but don't sell a single head. I'll see you in two or three weeks."

"Miss Starbuck?"

Jessie had been about to rein away, but now she stopped and looked back at Joe who said, "I just want to say for myself and the boys that we'll be all right. It's *you* we're

105

worried about. Don't give us and this herd of cattle a second thought."

Jessie was gratified by their genuine concern. You could always hire men to work for wages, but you couldn't buy loyalty and friendship. "When this is over and the cattle are sold, I'm going to take you boys up to Virginia City and treat you to a fine dinner. Then, I'll give you each a hundred dollar bonus, and you can tree that town if you've a mind."

The three cowboys beamed and nodded their heads with appreciation as Jessie rode away.

The road to Virginia City and the Comstock forked east about five miles south of Reno. It followed up Six Mile Canyon into rugged piñon, juniper and sagebrush country. Sun was a little on the thin side, but his long confinement in the cattle car made him eager to stretch his legs. Jessie let the palomino run until he was winded and the road grew windy and narrow. Huge ore and freight wagons formed an almost solid line up and down the mountainside, and the colorful language of the teamsters turned Jessie's ears red. There was also a solid stream of miners eagerly pushing on to Virginia City.

The queen city of the Comstock was named after one of the lode's first discoverers, a miner named Old Virginny. It seems the man was riding his burro around drunk, and the poor animal finally got tired of Old Virginny and bucked him off. Landing on rocks and breaking his precious bottle of whiskey, to the great hilarity of his peers, the old prospector attempted to salvage his dignity by raising his shattered bottle and crying, "I hereby christen this place, Virginny City!"

The name stuck, and by 1860 fortunes were being made. Hard-rock miners were swarming to this desolate

106

part of Nevada from all over the world. Jessie had not visited the Comstock for nearly five years, and when she finally topped a grade and looked down on the city, she was awed by its size and the amount of activity she saw.

St. Mary's in the Mountains, with its majestic white spire rising over the city, was the focal point, but other huge mansions and mine operations dotted the harsh landscape. The main thoroughfare, "C" Street, was clogged with wagon traffic, and it was now almost a mile long and reputed to be fronted by an even hundred saloons. Jessie pulled Sun off to the side of the road and let the animal catch its breath in the clear but thin mountain air. She was impressed by the dozens of huge mining operations that were scattered out at the base of Sun Mountain. There towering scaffolds and great tin sheds supported and protected the mighty steam engines that labored day and night over tunnels plunging straight down over a thousand feet into the hard rock. She heard the Virginia and Truckee Railroad engine's shrill blast lift over the town and saw the locomotive laboring up Gold Hill Canyon from Carson City.

Sadly, both the Protestant and Catholic cemeteries had tripled in size since her last visit. Hundreds of marble headstones glistened in the sunlight. It was late afternoon, and the shadows were quickly lengthening. Jessie remembered how it suddenly got chilly when the sun went down behind the Sierras.

Moving on, she rode down toward Virginia City, passing the Sierra Nevada, the Union and immensely profitable Ophir mining companies. When she came to the sheriff's office, just two doors down from *The Territorial Enterprise* newspaper building, Jessie dismounted and tied her horse at the hitching rail. The street and sidewalk were jammed with miners, and she received a good many whistles. Actually, in a town this full of men, she'd have had to be mighty ugly not to have received some male attention.

The sheriff's office was a solid brick structure. The moment she walked inside, she had a sense of neatness and efficiency. A tall, handsome young man with a sweeping blonde mustache and a deputy's badge was sitting at his desk. When he saw Jessie, he dropped his feet to the floor and stood up with a smile. "My, I hope I can be of some service to you, Miss..."

"Starbuck," Jessie said. "I'd like to see the sheriff."

"I'm afraid he's in the hospital. Gunshot wounds."

"Serious?"

"Yep. But he'll pull through. It seems a few of the miners we've arrested in the past wanted to get even. They bushwhacked Dick, but he managed to crawl under the boardwalk and return fire until I got to him."

"And then?"

"The bushwhackers will all be buried tomorrow morning," he said. "I guess I'm acting sheriff until Dick comes back—if he wants to come back. He's been shot, stabbed and beat over the head with bottles more times than he can count."

"It sounds like being a sheriff on the Comstock is dangerous."

The tall man nodded. He was fair-skinned, and his eyes were a pale slate gray and quite unusual. "It's worse than Abilene or Dodge City ever thought about being. Every eight hours there's another shift of miners coming up from the shafts, and all they want to do is drink and fight. There's nothing else to do except gamble and... well, you know."

Jessie saw the deputy blush. "I've come all the way from Texas to help a friend solve the murder of his wife. I don't even know where he lives, so I'll start by asking you."

"What's this fella's name?"

"Grant Sawyer."

The deputy took a deep breath and expelled it slowly. He shook his head and pursed his lips. "I'm afraid you came all the way from Texas for nothin', Miss Starbuck. You see, Grant Sawyer died a week ago Sunday."

Jessie was not easily shocked, but the news hit her like a hammer between the eyes. She was stunned.

The deputy took her arm. "Here," he said, "sit down in my chair. I'll get you a glass of water or something."

"Brandy," she said. "I'd like a shot of brandy."

"Yes, ma'am! I just happen to have some for emergencies and cold winter nights. It's not the best, but it'll steady you. I'm sorry about your friend. I should have given you the news a little easier."

Jessie took the brandy, only half listening to him. She could not believe that Sarah and Grant were both dead. They had been such good, gentle people. Sarah had been working for the Crossfire Mining Company, and her last letters had seemed so enthusiastic, so full of life. Grant had been an assayer when he had first arrived on the Comstock, then he'd become a mining consultant. He had always been interested in geology and engineering. They had probably not been getting rich, but they were happy and in love. And now, to hear that they were both dead. What a tragedy!

She finished the brandy and then declined another shot. Getting her emotions under control, she said, "Tell me about their deaths."

"All right," the deputy said. "But first I need to know how you fit into this."

109

Jessie did not mind explaining. The lawman's job was to know the reasons why people asked about murder. "I was Sarah's best friend during the years we were growing up. Grant Sawyer was like my brother until he got old enough to think he didn't want to be a brother anymore. We . . . well, we just stayed friends. What is your name?"

"Deputy Tom Cutter. I'm sorry about your friends. I hardly knew them but I worked on the case, and everyone I talked to thought they were both fine people. Both died badly, I'm afraid. Mrs. Sawyer took violently ill and passed over before a doctor could get to her bedside."

"What was the cause of death?"

"No one is sure. The doctor said he had never seen anything quite like it."

"What's his name?"

"Butterman. Doctor Amos Butterman. Got an office up on "A" street next to the Storey County Courthouse. He's the county coroner."

"But he doesn't know why Sarah died?" Jessie asked.

"Nope. At least, that's what he told me. Said it might have been from natural causes. A lot of people die of natural causes up here."

"Did Grant die of 'natural causes?'"

"No, ma'am. I wish he had. I'm afraid Grant died of violent causes. You see, he fell about sixteen hundred feet down a mine shaft."

Jessie reached for the brandy and poured another shot. She was tired and worn down from her long journey and nearly at the end of her reserves. It must have shown because the deputy said, "You look a little peaky, Miss Starbuck. Maybe I ought to escort you over to a nice hotel."

"I'll be all right," she said. "Which mine shaft did Grant tumble down?"

"The Bonanza Unlimited. They paid all funeral expenses, and it was first class. They're both buried out in the Protestant cemetery. If you want, I'll take you out and show you their graves tomorrow."

"I can find them," she said. "Did anyone think to ask how Grant tumbled down a mine shaft?"

The deputy looked away. "It was an accident," he said. "I investigated and it was accidental. Happens all too often."

"Grant was a very careful man," she said. "I don't believe he made many mistakes. How was it an accident?"

"I'd rather not say."

Jessie stood up and looked the deputy right in the eye. "Mr. Cutter, if you're trying to hide something from me, then please don't!"

"All right," he said with a shrug of his shoulders. "Grant Sawyer died from massive head injuries. In fact, by the time he'd bounced off the walls for a thousand feet, he didn't have much of a head left."

Jessie stood up and walked to the door, trying hard not to visualize what a man would look like after such a terrible fall. At the door, she stopped and said, "Is there anything more you can tell me?"

"Yeah," the deputy said. "But you can go to the newspaper office and ask Dan DeQuille to dig you out a copy of the account he wrote on it. It'll give you all the gory details I'd rather not talk about."

She nodded. "Thank you."

"Miss Starbuck? Is there some logical reason why you're so curious about the cause of death?"

Jessie decided to be honest with him. She was going to need his help and cooperation and therefore could not afford to seem evasive. "Yes, there is. I have a telegram in

111

my pocket. Perhaps you'd like to take a look at it."

He came forward to take the telegram. He read it swiftly and his expression grew hard. "I don't know what the hell he was talking about when he says his wife was murdered. Could be he was drunk."

"Grant *never* took a drink in his life."

The deputy stepped back and shook his head. "I beg your pardon, Miss Starbuck, but he was drinking on the night he fell down the mine shaft. People seen him drunk; he carried a flask of whiskey in his coat pocket and reeked of liquor. I know. I had to see and smell him. It took two hours to get the man up to the surface."

Jessie swallowed. "Grant Sawyer was raised a Mormon. I repeat—he *never* drank."

They locked eyes and the deputy finally looked away. "Miss Starbuck, are you sure you don't want me to take you to a hotel for the night?"

"No. I've my horse to stable first."

"Use George Austin's Stable down at the end of the street. The Occidental Hotel is the best we have for respectable women."

"Thank you."

He stepped outside with her. "You sure you don't want me to take you down to the cemetery tomorrow? Might make you feel better to visit them."

"No," she said pointedly, "it wouldn't. But I appreciate your kind offer anyway. I'll be talking to you again tomorrow. I'll have even more questions before I leave Virginia City."

"Start with Dan DeQuille and *The Territorial Enterprise*," he said again. "Then tomorrow, you might want to talk to old Doc Butterman."

Jessie nodded. "You can bet I will," she vowed. "He'll be one of the first on my list."

Jessie untied her palomino and then mounted the animal while the deputy watched. He said, "Mighty fast looking animal there. A little thin, though."

"I know," she said before riding away.

Chapter 12

The two-storied, brick *Territorial Enterprise* building was not especially imposing, yet Jessie knew that the newspaper's tremendous circulation was world-wide. So great was the Comstock's influence on gold and silver values that investors on the eastern seaboard, as well as in Europe and the Orient, subscribed to it and read it like their gospel. It was also very "lively" and had quite a reputation for its bizarre and extremely humorous accounts of Comstock life, written by Dan DeQuille and his famous predecessor, Mark Twain.

But Jessie wasn't in any mood for humor when she entered the office of *The Territorial Enterprise* and asked to meet Dan DeQuille. She was directed back near the Washington printing presses where she located the famed Comstock reporter working at a huge roll-top desk that must have had twenty pigeon-holes for various stories being filed. DeQuille was a tall, thin, slightly-stooped man, who was very serious looking. Had Jessie not read his humorous columns many a time and the serious ones that qualified the reporter as being the resident expert on Comstock mining and speculation, she would have guessed him an undertaker in his somber, rumpled black suit and soiled white shirt.

"Mr. DeQuille, I need to talk to you," she said extending her hand.

He looked up and was about to say he had a deadline to meet when he saw her face and changed his mind. "My pleasure!" he said, popping out of his seat and grabbing a chair for her.

Very quickly, Jessie introduced herself and stated her mission. She ended by handing Grant Sawyer's telegram to DeQuille and saying, "As you can see, Grant Sawyer did not think his wife died of any natural causes. He thought she was murdered, and he must have realized his own life was in danger or he wouldn't have asked for my help."

"But why *your* help? The sheriff and his deputy are both capable men. Honest and probably even uncorruptable. And most importantly, they were here."

It was a good question, and one that Jessie had asked herself more than a few times. "I'm not sure I know the answer to that," she admitted. "Unless it was because Grant either didn't trust the law in Virginia City, or else he felt that they wouldn't listen to him and take his suspicions seriously. But I take them very seriously. It's like I told Deputy Cutter. Grant Sawyer was a very prudent and careful man. He was a Mormom—"

"Now wait a minute," DeQuille said, wagging his head back and forth in protest. "I knew the man, and he never attended services with the Mormons."

"I'll amend what I said," Jessie added quickly. "He might have fallen away from his church, but he retained his high moral values. To my knowledge, he never drank, swore or used tobacco. And the idea of him being drunk and falling down a mine shaft is ridiculous."

DeQuille frowned. "When I wrote the story, I have to

115

admit, I was a bit puzzled by the liquor for I never saw Grant take a drink either. And, on the Comstock, that's a very unusual characteristic. Half of us are drunks, the other half aspire to be."

Jessie smiled for she knew that DeQuille was anything but a drunk. He had a gift for exaggeration and a wonderful writing style that was admired wherever his columns were in print.

"Can I read your account of the death?"

"Of course. But it's simply an obituary. Because I knew the man personally and because his wife had such a short while before his own untimely demise, I thought it would make good print."

Jessie said nothing. She waited while the Comstock reporter went to a huge stack of newspapers and finally located the one he was searching for. "Here," DeQuille said, finding the page and placing a long, ink-stained finger on the column.

Jessie was disappointed that the column had so few details. Basically, it reiterated everything she had learned from Deputy Cutter. The only new fact was that Grant Sawyer had apparently been discharged as a mining consultant from the Bonanza Limited only a couple of days before his fall.

"If he had been discharged," Jessie asked, "then why was he in the Bonanza Unlimited's mine shaft?"

DeQuille picked up his pipe. "Do you mind if I smoke in your presence?"

"Not one bit."

The newspaperman nodded, and his eyes drifted to some spot high on the wall. For perhaps a full minute, he seemed quite lost in his own thoughts as he filled his pipe and packed it with his forefinger. Appearing to make a decision that satisfied him, he lit it and exhaled. "That was the one question that did not seem to have an answer," he said. "What I was told by the company officials was that Grant Sawyer had 'gone over the edge' with grief after his wife's death. He was unreliable and therefore had to be discharged. The only thing that those mining officials could theorize was that losing his job had pushed Mr. Sawyer completely over the brink of sanity. That he'd been on his way down into the Bonanza Unlimited to wreck some mischief or worse."

"I don't believe a word of it!"

"You should know that the sheriff found fuses, blasting caps and matches in Mr. Sawyer's pockets. Down at each station, there are hundreds of pounds of blasting powder. No one except the blasting foreman is allowed to take matches down to the lower levels. Grant most certainly knew that rule. Yet, it appears he got drunk and violated the rule. I'm afraid the case for attempted sabotage is very strong, Miss Starbuck. Of course, due to the fact that he died, nothing was said of either the matches or the blasting caps. What would be the use of casting aspersions upon a dead man?"

Jessie was shaking with anger when she stood up to leave. "Mr. DeQuille, though you haven't said as much, I have the impression that your own highly-developed instincts are a jingle here. You know something is slightly amiss."

DeQuille shrugged. "Miss Starbuck. We are world-famed here on the Comstock. Men come and many die. There are murders almost daily. Revenge, love, betrayal. They are the reason I stay here on this mountainside. Where on earth could a reporter find more to write about?"

"Please make your point."

"Very well. My point is that murder is common here. I ask questions, the sheriff asks questions, his deputy asks questions. But we've not the time or the resources to persist and to ask the deep questions that, say, a small town lawman or reporter would ask. Everyday I have big news to write about. Death is routine, even murder is commonplace."

"I understand," Jessie told him. "But Sarah and Grant Sawyer were not 'common' in any sense of the word. They were special to me. I'm going to find out the real reason they died, and then I'll give you a story, Mr. DeQuille. One that will sell plenty of newspapers."

He took the pipe out of his mouth and smiled through tobacco-stained teeth. "And then I will be very grateful. I wish you good luck. I will help you when and if you begin to find real evidence. Until then, good day."

Jessie walked up the steep Union Street and then turned left on "A" Street. She passed the Storey County Courthouse and entered the medical office of Dr. Amos Butterman.

"Be right out!" he called when a small jingle bell attached to the door announced her entry.

Jessie waited patiently for almost a quarter of an hour before the doctor bustled out to see her. He had a round face, small, porcine lips and was quite rotund. He might have been in his thirties or his fifties, it was impossible to say. His eyes were deeply set behind thick, wire-rimmed glasses and still he blinked myopically. "My," he said, studying her in a very non-clinical manner, "you certainly do not appear unwell."

"I'm not," Jessie said.

"Then what may I do for you?"

"I want to talk to you about two deaths. Those of Mr. and Mrs. Grant Sawyer."

The doctor's friendly attitude vanished. "I'm afraid I

118

don't have time for that. I've a living to make, just like anyone else. Good day."

Jessie was not about to let him go. She followed him to a door leading back into his examination room, and when she entered, she saw a totally nude cadaver that was undergoing an autopsy. For a moment, the smell of embalming solutions and other pungent chemicals almost gagged her.

Butterman saw her color change and he smiled with malice. "Something upsetting you, dear girl?"

Jessie forced herself to look away from the cadaver. The deceased was in his twenties and had been shot twice in the face. The doctor had entered the cadaver's cranium and was extracting the lead slugs, probably for evidence against the man's killer.

"I'm fine," Jessie managed to say, riveting her eyes on Butterman's thick lenses. "But I insist on knowing about the Sawyers. What kind of a diagnosis is 'natural causes' for a twenty-five year old woman in perfect health?"

"Perfect health?" He went back to work, his pudgy fingers gripping a scalpel and forceps as he began to probe the soft gray matter of the brain. "Who can say anyone is in perfect health? There is no such thing as perfect health. Children die of unexplainable causes. Adults are victims of their heredities. I have seen men strong enough to lift a horse suddenly topple over dead from a busted vessel in the brain, or a defective heart."

"Yes," Jessie said, fuming at his nonsensical theories in the face of murder. "But you found nothing defective in Sarah Sawyer. Admit it."

He looked down at his hands and then dug out a lead slug. He dropped the slug into a kidney-shaped metal basin and then he looked up and said, "Actually, I did see signs of arterial disease."

"Of what!"

119

"Failure of neural arteries. A major cranial artery was defective and it leaked. This caused pressure in the brain which gave the classic symptoms of vomiting and nausea. What seemed to be an abdominal-related death, perhaps one caused by food poisoning, was actually caused by the failure of a cerebral artery."

"I don't believe a word of what you've said," Jessie told the man.

Butterman shrugged his round shoulders. "My medical findings are on public record. It's a county-paid autopsy, just like this one. Check the records next door in the court-house."

"I will." Jessie was furious and also helpless because she knew that there wasn't a thing she could do to refute Dr. Butterman's medical findings. Sarah was dead and buried and that was the end of it. "What about Grant Sawyer?"

"Almost beheaded," the doctor said. "There was certainly no cause for an autopsy. He was drunk and he fell out of the wire cage that lowers miners up and down Bonanza Unlimited's mine shaft. There are dozens of witnesses. Now, unless you have some morbid preoccupation with watching this sort of thing, I suggest that you get out of my office."

Dismissed and defeated for the moment, Jessie had no choice but to leave but before doing so, she said, "I think they were both murdered and that you are very aware of that fact. And I'll tell you this, Dr. Butterman. I just might hire medical doctors to come over from San Francisco and watch your every move. I have a feeling you are a party to murder."

His hand jumped up, the scalpel crimson and evil looking. "Get out of here! Get out this very minute."

Jessie looked into those blinking little eyes, and she

knew she had touched some truth because he'd reacted so violently. She felt a small triumph. "I'll see you again," she promised. "Most likely in a courtroom."

The doctor moved around the examining table toward her, but Jessie retreated and left his office. Outside, the air was fresh of chemicals, and after she had walked a safe distance down the street, she stopped, breathed deeply and felt her head clear. From her vantage point, she could see across the lower streets of Virginia City out to the east for miles and miles. Beyond the hoisting works, the huge piles of mine tailings, and the railroad line, there was nothing but open country. Rolling, rotted brown hills without water or grass. It was high desert country, washboarded by one sun-blasted mountain range after another.

Her gaze moved in closer to the cemeteries, which were about two miles away. Jessie started walking toward them. She'd find no more of an answer at Sarah or Grant's gravesite than she had in Dr. Butterman's examining room, but she needed time to think. To decide which string to start unraveling in the best hope of learning the answer to this Comstock riddle.

Maybe, from the grave, Sarah or Grant could somehow help her.

Chapter 13

It was late afternoon when she left the Protestant section of the Virginia City Cemetery with its tall, wrought-iron gates and stark vistas. Jessie had had no trouble finding the gravesites of her friends, and after a long communion with them, she had left feeling somehow better and more confident that she would be able to bring the killers of her friends to justice.

Walking up "D" Street, Jessie stopped at the Crossfire Mining Company and decided that it was a good place to start asking questions. Like most of the more prosperous Comstock mines, this one was patroled by guards with sawed off shotguns. It was their job to check the miners going off shift and to make sure that they did not steal gold or silver ore.

"Good afternoon," she said, greeting the two stony-faced men who had been watching her approach from the cemetery. "I'd like to see whoever is in charge."

They studied her carefully. "What for?" the larger of the two asked. "You want a job, or what?"

The other man whoofed a laugh as if it was the best joke he'd heard in weeks. "Hell, I'll give her a job, right over in those bushes right now! How much for good time, honey?"

"More than you'll make in your lifetime, you foul-mouthed oaf."

The man's laughter choked in his throat. "Why, you can't talk to me thata way!"

He started to grab her, but Jessie stepped back. She wasn't wearing her gun on her shapely hip, but she was armed with a derringer and now she pulled it out of her dress and cocked it. "It's two shots, and I don't often miss at this range," she said, making certain that they both understood she meant business.

"What the hell do you want!"

"I want to know the name of your mining superintendent."

"Mike Colson."

"Go get him," Jessie said. "Now."

The guard wavered. The shotgun was resting in his hands, and it would only have taken a second to shift it and fire. But Jessie's hand and voice were rock-steady, and the gun she held was a .45 and that made a big hole in a man's chest.

"All right," he said, "I'll go. Frank, you stay right here and don't let her past you."

Frank nodded. He was younger and looked smarter. Maybe he realized that he wasn't going to do anything to stop Jessie as long as she had a derringer pointed only inches from his face.

Jessie watched the foul-mouthed guard march toward the big, tin-roofed building that was the standard for mining company offices and machinery works. She could see smoke funneling out of two chimneys, and she could hear the clanking of the heavy machinery hidden inside the huge tin building.

"What do you want to see Mr. Colson for?" the guard asked, trying to act as if the gun was not pointed at him.

"I don't think that's any of your business."

The man flustered and his neck reddened. "Well . . . well I'm being paid to ask that question! It's my job to know everyone's business that comes here."

"But it's not your job to insult visitors," Jessie said.

"I didn't make that wise crack about going into the bushes, Ernie did!"

"You laughed."

He swallowed noisily. Toed the dirt. "You don't need to keep that pistol pointed at me. I'd never blast a woman."

Jessie supposed she could trust him. She backed out of reach and lowered the derringer to her side, but she did not put it away. Her wariness was not lost on the young guard. "You ain't a very trusting woman, are you?"

"Not with your kind of men. Did you know the Sawyers?"

"Sure!" he said, apparently eager to switch the subject. "Everybody did. They both worked here, but Mr. Sawyer quit a couple years ago."

"Are you sure?"

"Yeah. Guess he didn't want to work in the same place as his wife. Maybe it was company policy or something. Anyway, Sawyer tried to start his own company. Had a claim but not enough cash to buy the machinery he needed. So he sold out and went to work for Bonanza Unlimited right over there."

Jessie looked to where he pointed his finger. "You mean, this first mining company down the road?"

"Yep. It was so close that, sometimes, Mr. and Mrs. Sawyer would get together in one office or the other and take their meals together. They was mighty close. Everybody liked 'em."

"Someone at the Bonanza didn't like Grant, or he wouldn't have been fired."

The guard shifted uncomfortably. "They say he got drunk and stayed drunk after his wife died. I don't know about that. I seen him one afternoon down in Silver City, and he was sober as a judge. Mighty serious looking too. But after losin' his wife, I guess he had good reason to look serious."

"Did you ever hear him talk about this mine, or the Bonanza Unlimited?"

"On, no, ma'am! Anybody like that, or an assayer, anybody talks about what they know and they'd get their heads busted or worse. Them people are like priests hearing a confession. They don't tell nothing if they want to stay in business."

"I see."

A silver-haired man of about fifty came marching up the well-trod path from the tin building. He was dressed in a suit and tie, the working uniform of mining management, and he was annoyed. "My name is Mike Colson. What's this I hear about you pulling a gun on my guards."

"It seemed they needed a lesson in manners, Mr. Colson. Unless it's your company's policy to humiliate and degrade ladies."

Colson blinked. Maybe he wasn't accustomed to being spoken to in that manner. But at any rate, he shook his head. "What can I do for you?"

"I'd like a moment of your time. It concerns Sarah Sawyer."

"Come on down to my office," he said, shooting a hard glance at his guards and saying, "I'll speak to you boys about this later."

Jessie and the mining superintendent walked briskly down to the tin building with the sound of the machinery getting louder and louder. When they entered the building, the noise was so loud it was almost impossible to talk.

Jessie had a glimpse of a ponderous winding reel and a jungle of heavy machinery before she was ushered through a heavily insulated door into the company's surprisingly plush business offices where Jessie saw three women and several young male clerks busily working. Colson had his own private office, and it was as nice as anything you would find in any major corporation. The paneling was imported from the Black Forest of Germany and so thick that even though they could still hear the heavy thump-thump of the big machinery and feel a slight tremble in the flooring, they did not have to shout to carry on a normal conversation.

"All right," Colson said moving behind his big desk and taking a seat after motioning her to an expensive leather chair. "What can I tell you about Mrs. Sawyer except that we were grieved by her sudden death? She worked here almost four years. She was kind, loyal and efficient. She was irreplaceable. Now, who are you?"

"I was a very good friend of the Sawyers," Jessie said. "I'm investigating what I believe was their murder."

"You are out of your mind," he said. "Mrs. Sawyer died of natural causes. There's an autopsy report on file at the county courthouse."

"I don't need to read it, I've already talked to Dr. Butterman. I told him the same thing that I told you. Grant Sawyer believed his wife was murdered and that his own life was in danger. He sent a telegram to me stating that fact. I came, but obviously too late. All I can do now is to find out why they were murdered, and by whom."

"Miss . . ."

"Starbuck. Jessica Starbuck of Texas."

"Ah-ha!" he exclaimed. "I should have guessed. Sarah spoke of you many times. She was proud to have been your close friend. The fact that you came all the way from

Texas to see her grave is, in itself, a tribute to that friendship."

Jessie did not like this man. He was too smooth, too glib, too ready with a compliment cleverly delivered to divert the conversation. "I also brought a herd of cattle I plan to sell on the Comstock."

"Wonderful. The price of beef up here is astronomical. You should make a killing." His expression changed. "I'm sorry. Under the circumstances of your visit, I guess 'killing' is a poor choice of words."

"What did Sarah do for you?"

"The books. Filing. Correspondence. The usual. She was in charge of our office records."

Jessie looked out through Colson's glass office windows into the main business area. Everything she saw was new and expensive. It sure was deceptive to stand outside the claim, look at the huge tin barn and imagine it housed such expensive offices and machinery. But then, maybe that was the way all these successful mines operated. Maybe it was their intent to give the impression of hardship and austerity so that their labor union was inclined to ask for smaller raises. Jessie doubted that the rank-and-file miners ever saw the inside of this place.

"Miss Starbuck. May I ask what you are after with questions about Mrs. Sawyer's work here?"

"I'm not sure," she said.

Colson stood up. "I'd love to chat with you about Sarah, really I would. But unfortunately, I have a mine to run and there are always problems."

"How deep are you?"

"Sixteen hundred feet." He shook his head. "I doubt we'll be able to go much deeper. The temperature at that level is 130 degrees. We ship down a hundred pounds of ice per man per eight hour shift and they still spend most of their time gasping like beached carp. The labor costs at that level are kill . . . are trememdous. The air is bad, we have pumps going twenty-four hours a day trying to keep the water level down."

"You must be finding ore, or you wouldn't be there."

"We manage," he said with a tolerant smile. "Just barely."

Jessie looked around the room. "I'd say, from the looks of these offices, you do a sight better than 'just manage.' One more question and then I'll go."

"Very well. You can ask anything, but I'll not give you insider information."

"All I want to know is this. Did Grant Sawyer ever work for you as a mining consultant?"

"For us?"

Jessie knew the man had heard and understood her question the first time. "Yes."

"No. No, I'm sure he did not."

"That's very interesting," she said. "You've been more help than you know."

She started for the door, but he held her up a moment. "Why did you say it was interesting?"

Jessie smiled. "I'd just heard otherwise."

"Oh. Well, I guess there are probably some people who thought he worked as a consultant for us. I mean —his wife was on the payroll and he visited her once or twice on the premises, but he didn't make a habit of it. You see, he worked for our neighbor and competitor, Bonanza Unlimited. A mining consultant or assayer can't afford to get chummy with more than one mining outfit. We all have our trade secrets."

"What does that mean?"

"Secrecy is a part of doing business on the Comstock. A very important part. For example, when we hit a vein of pure silver or gold, we certainly don't want to tell our competitors its exact location. We would much rather mine it to the subterranean borders of our claim and then, hopefully, buy the mine next door at a reasonable price."

"'Reasonable,'" Jessie said, wanting to make sure she understood, "meaning that you want to keep your competitors in the dark about new discoveries so that you can buy them out far more cheaply."

"Of course! I know that you're a very successful businesswoman. Surely, you must understand the winning strategies of commerce. Also, there are hundreds of very small claims filed on the Comstock. They are owned by ignorant, under-financed miners who cannot afford to really mine the way the Comstock must be mined for a profit. So, larger operations like ourselves, simply buy them up as they become available."

"For a pittance." Jessie could not help a note of scorn from creeping into her voice.

"Not necessarily," he said, bristling at the veiled slight. "No one up here is stupid. We have to pay thousands of dollars for claims that would have sold a few years ago for a couple of hundred."

"But the mineral rights to those claims will yield millions of dollars to a big company like this."

"They can, if we know where the veins run. And of course, that is never an exact science. On the Comstock, the veins seem to dip and waver unpredictably. And there are big pockets of pure gold or silver that are extremely hard to find."

Colson smiled and said. "But I've talked too much."

"Yes," Jessie said. "From your standpoint, you really have.'"

His jaw dropped two inches, and before he could get angry, Jessie excused herself and left.

Out at the gates, the two guards practically bowed when she passed. "Have a good day, ma'am," the larger one said.

"I will. By the way. You said Grant Sawyer worked here once. How long ago?"

"Little over a year."

"Thank you." Jessie headed down the dirt street walking fast. She wanted to visit Bonanza Unlimited. She had some very interesting questions to ask.

The man who stood before her had introduced himself as Dirk Pardee, and he was not very nice. "I don't know what you think you're doing coming around here asking a bunch of dumb questions. I don't owe you any explanations. You got no right to come on this property, so just turn around and shag it on down the road."

Jessie was furious, so angry that she had to be careful not to speak out of turn. "I doubt very much if you own this mining company," she said. "And I imagine it will be pretty easy to find out who does. When I do, I'll be back and you will be helpful to me."

"You're a busy-body," he said. "A damn rich one and a damn good looking one, but a busy-body all the same. I don't know what you're asking all these questions about Grant Sawyer for, but it'll do you no good."

"Who told you I've been asking questions?"

He was momentarily at loss for words. "The word is out," he growled, waving his hand as if it did not matter. "Besides, that don't matter. What matters is that Sawyer was fired—by me—and then he tried to come back and get even. The way I see it, the guy deserved to fall. He was gonna blow up this mine and take a lot of good men with him."

"The way you see it is wrong, Mr. Pardee. Someone set

Grant up. They must have poured whiskey on his clothes and then pushed him out of the cage."

"That's crazy talk," Pardee said. "It's the kind of loose talk that can get a person in trouble."

Jessie looked right into his eyes. He was of average height, with course features, unruly hair and the red, bulbous nose of a heavy drinker. "Is that a threat?"

"It's a warning," he said. "Stay out of my hair. I won't let you on the property. Period."

"You could save us both a lot of time by answering just a couple of simple questions," Jessie said. "Did Grant work here?"

"Anybody can tell you he did."

"Was he a major stockholder?"

"Hell, no!"

"Is this mine and the Crossfire owned by the same people?"

"Get out of here!"

There was enough venom in his voice to tell her she just might have hit upon something. She wondered how he seemed to have known she was coming at the very minute she had. He'd seemed to be almost waiting at the entrance with his guard.

"Do you have a telegraph line buried between Bonanza Unlimited and the Crossfire? Did Mr. Colson send a message warning you I was coming right over?"

Pardee looked mad enough to kill her. "You step between their claim and ours, you're trespassing and could be shot," he hissed. "It'd be a terrible waste, but around here, we don't put up with snoopy people. We put 'em under the ground about six feet deep. Now git!"

"I'll be back," she vowed. "And the next time I come, you'll either have been fired, or ordered to show me this mining operation, from top to bottom."

Jessie left with a gut-feeling that she had made a correct guess about the two mines being in direct communications. That flew directly in the face of all the talk of secrecy she had heard was so precious on the Comstock. If the mines were connected, and if Sarah and Grant had worked for them, there were too many connections to be ignored.

She didn't yet have enough information to fit the pieces of the puzzle together, but she knew they had to fit. Jessie realized that she needed help. She would wire her attorneys in San Francisco and have them check on the legal ownership of the two mines. She'd also have them research the board of directors and any other major stockholders. If she could prove that the two mines were financially connected, it would tell her something. She could not decide exactly what it would tell her, but she would worry about that later.

Chapter 14

The next morning found Jessie striding purposefully toward the telegraph office. "C" Street was as busy as usual, and a stagecoach rolled past. Jessie heard a passenger whistle at her, but she paid the man no mind. She was accustomed to whistles. She had learned it was better not to acknowledge them or she'd only encourage bold advances. Besides, she was thinking about the telegraph that she would send to San Francisco, and then she wondered if the information she sought just might be on file in Carson City, the State Capitol. Of course it would be!

Jessie abruptly turned and headed back toward the Occidental Hotel. She'd change into a riding habit and then have Sun readied. It would be quicker to ride her horse than to go down to the V. & T. Railroad and wait around for the next train to Carson City.

"Hey! Are you so used to whistles that you don't even look up anymore!" a man called.

Jessie turned to see Black Snake Charley come swinging up to her side. He was lean and long-legged and appeared as if he hadn't a care in the world. Fresh off the stage, his hat was cocked back at a jaunty angle and he looked as happy as a man going fishing. He was grinning when he took her hand, raised it to his lips and kissed it. "Your knight in tarnished armor is once again at your service."

Jessie was glad to see him. "I could use a friend," she said, counting the days when she expected to see Ki again.

"Then you got me."

"How much do you charge for escort service to Carson City?"

"A dollar a mile," he said, meaning it. "From here to there is plenty rough country. Lots of hard men and there could be trouble in Gold Hill Canyon."

"If you can handle a gun the way you can handle that blacksnake," she said motioning to the whip that seemed almost a part of him, "then you're well worth the money. Meet me at George Austin's Stable down at the end of the street in about twenty minutes. I'm never late, and I detest waiting on anyone."

"We taking a buggy or horses?"

"Horses," Jessie said. "I'm a Texas ranch woman, remember?"

"That's right. Okay, but you'll have to rent me a nag and a saddle. I don't have one of my own."

"Take your pick of what's available and tell the stable to charge me. Anyway, I thought you had business in Ogden."

"I did. Finished it early and took a stage for Nevada early the next morning. I remembered you saying you were coming up here. A woman like you stands out in a crowd, Miss Jessie. I saw you walking down the street and didn't even wait for my stage to hold up."

"Well, I'm glad you came. I've got big troubles here in Virginia City. I'll tell you about them on the way down to Carson City."

They parted company, and Jessie continued on to the Occidental Hotel. She hurried up the stairs to the second floor and used her key to let herself into her room. No sooner had she shut the door behind her and started to turn around, than a powerful hand clamped itself over her mouth. She was lifted up and thrown to her bed face down.

Jessie tried to scream and to bite the hand, but it was gloved. All she could sink her teeth into was cowhide. She had the impression there were two men in her room, and both of them were on top of her, pushing her face into the soft bed comforter until she could not breathe. She struggled but was pinned so roughly that she could do nothing but wiggle her legs, and even they were being tied together.

Suddenly the hand pulled away, Jessie managed to raise her head a little and take a deep breath of air. It saved her life for she had almost been suffocated. But then, a dirty rag was jammed into her mouth before she could take another breath and shout. A bandana was then forced between her teeth and pulled back behind her head and tied. It was all Jessie could do to keep for choking to death. Her hands were bound behind her back and a blindfold was used to cover her eyes. In less than a minute, she was bound, blinded and silenced. Whoever the men were, they'd done this before, and they were professionals.

"Turn her over and let her breathe," one of them said, just as Jessie thought she was going to faint.

She was grabbed and rudely rolled over onto her back. One of the men said, "Boy, ain't she got a body, though! Why don't we just untie her legs and . . ."

"No! We got our orders. Let's get her out of here."

Jessie felt herself being lifted, then thrown over a man's shoulder. A very big man's shoulder.

"It's clear in the hallway to the back stairs," the other said. "Let's go!"

She was rushed down the hallway, out the back door

and down the back stairs. "Hey, there's someone down there looking at us!"

"Let it ride. He'll keep his mouth shut!"

A moment later, she was thrown into a buckboard and a smelly tarp was pulled over her. The buckboard started off with a jerk and she heard one of the men say, "You try to roll out back there, I'll kill you. Pretty and young as you are, I'll still do it!"

Jessie believed the man. She was lying on a thin blanket and had no idea where they were taking her or for what purpose. Everything that came to mind was bad. She had only been on the Comstock a few days and had made several enemies. Dr. Butterman, Mike Colson, and Dirk Pardee were prime candidates behind this kidnapping. They were all suspicious and probably working together. Who else? Certainly not Dan DeQuille. Perhaps the deputy. He was the only other one that knew her purpose for being on the Comstock.

And who could help her now? Not Ki, for his train was not due from Plum Creek until Wednesday. There was no one to help her, unless . . . unless it was Black Snake Charley and he never did anything without first wanting a guarantee of payment.

Black Snake Charley stood in front of the livery barn and attracted a large crowd of admirers as he practiced killing horseflies wherever they were foolish enough to land on the livery wall. He never missed, and no one in Virginia City had ever seen a whip move faster or pop louder. He was really getting warmed up and thinking about setting his hat out so people could actually show their appreciation when he remembered that Jessie had said she would come by soon.

"What time is it?" he shouted to no one in particular.

"Ten-forty," was the answer.

Black Snake wound up his bullwhip. He knew that the stage to Virginia City had been right on time, and it had arrived at ten o'clock. That meant Jessie was forty minutes late, and she wasn't the type to keep a man waiting. Maybe she was in trouble or someone was giving her grief.

"Show is over," he said. "Maybe I'll do it again sometime."

The spectators, mostly old men and foreigners with nothing to do that didn't cost money, wandered away while Black Snake headed for the Occidental Hotel.

"What's Miss Starbuck's room number?" he asked the hotel clerk.

The man had been reading the latest edition of *The Territorial Enterprise* featuring one of Dan DeQuille's latest spoofs. He was annoyed to be distracted. "I'm sorry. There are no men allowed upstairs. If you're expected, you may wait for your lady here in the lobby."

Black Snake had no intention of waiting in any lobby. He marched around the desk, slapped the newspaper aside and jerked the man out of his chair. "You little rodent," he hissed. "I asked you a question, and I'll have an answer or I'll have your gizzard!"

The clerk's eyes widened, and he stammered, "Number 204!"

Black Snake released the man and then picked up his newspaper. "I don't know why people have to always do things the hard way," he said with a sad shake of his head. "But you do."

He headed up the stairs taking them two at a time. When he reached the second story landing, he walked quickly until he came to Jessie's room, then he banged on the door. When there was no answer, he tried the knob and discovered it was unlocked. Stepping inside, he at once

137

saw the evidence of foul play. A chair was overturned, the bed was all messed up, and there were cigar butts ground into the carpet.

Black Snake whirled and headed back down the stairs on the run. He didn't even ask the clerk if he'd seen men go upstairs because whoever had abducted Jessie would have had to use stealth to get up to the room and then to get her safely out of the hotel.

He ran around to the back of the hotel and saw the fresh wheel tracks of a buckboard. He knelt in the soft dirt and saw the bootmarks. He knew this was where Jessie had been taken, but that was all he was sure of. The plain truth of things was that there was so much wagon traffic on the streets of Virginia City that he'd never be able to follow these tracks. Black Snake's heart beat heavily. He was afraid that he wasn't going to be a hell of a lot of help. There were probably a couple hundred buggies and buckboards with wheel widths like this running around every day.

"Mister, are you looking for the woman that they carried down those back stairs?"

Black Snake whirled to see a man. A very dirty, bewhiskered and disreputable looking man who swayed slightly on his feet.

"Yeah," he said, "I sure as hell am."

"Did you see her!"

"Uh-huh."

"Well who took her!"

"Cost you twenty dollars."

Black Snake jumped at the man and grabbed him by the collar. "I'll tear your head off if you don't tell me."

The man reeked of sweat and whiskey. "You can kill me, but I still ain't going to tell you," he muttered. "Without the twenty dollars for whiskey, I'd as soon be dead anyway."

Black Snake cussed. "All I got is eighteen dollars and fifty, maybe eight cents."

"Let's see the money."

Black Snake cussed again, and then he counted it out. It came up a nickel shy of being nineteen dollars and the man took it. Every last cent.

"All right!" he growled. "There's the money now tell me everything you saw back here."

"There was two of 'em. One big, one little. They had a pillowcase over her head, but she sure had pretty legs."

"What kind of a wagon?"

"Buckboard." The drunk licked his lips and started to walk away, but Black Snake grabbed him by the collar. "Describe it and the damned horses."

"Hell, man! It was just an ordinary old buckboard."

"That's not enough. Give me back the money or give me enough of a description to find her."

"All right! All right! There was two horses. A dapple gray and a sorrel. The big man was wearing a ten-gallon hat, like them damned Texas cowboys do, and he wore Mexican spurs. The littler guy had a beard and a shotgun. Now let go of me you broke sonofabitch!"

"One more question. Which way did they go?"

"Down toward Gold Canyon and Dayton on the Carson River. Now let go of me, for crissakes! Pick on someone your own size and age, damn you!"

Black Snake let the man go, who now made a beeline for the nearest saloon. In two hours, he'd have spent the whole twenty dollars and be too drunk to know his own name.

Black Snake headed for the livery at a run. The horses were saddled and ready to ride. He took a good buckskin and Jessie's palomino. He rode out fast, crossed "D" and "F" Streets and headed down Taylor Street passing over the railroad line and striking the road toward Dayton. By the time he had cleared town, he'd angered more than a few pedestrians and freighters with his wild riding, but he did not give a damn. He figured that whoever had taken Jessie might just intend to ransom her for money, but they might also be plain murderers.

As he galloped down the mountain road, he wondered how much money Jessie might be willing to part with for his heroics. Oh, he'd have tried to save her anyway, but it was sure a lot better to be rewarded for your efforts. Suddenly, he remembered that he'd forgotten to bring a gun. He glanced at Jessie's saddle and rifle boot but, of course, she'd not left a good rifle in the boot for someone to steal. It struck him pretty hard that he was chasing two desperate and armed kidnappers with no weapons except his whip and his old pocket knife. And while he figured he could take care of most things with a bullwhip, it still wasn't quite the match of a sawed off shotgun.

Black Snake tried to forget about the fact that he was unarmed. He rode on and on until he came down to the high desert and could see the line of green cottonwood trees along the Carson River. Then, just as he was starting to wonder whether to turn left or right, he caught a glimpse of the buckboard as it disappeared into the trees. It looked as if it was heading west onto the property of one of the many sawmills that lined the river between Carson City and Dayton.

Black Snake rode off at an angle, and when he came to the river, he was a good quarter mile below the sawmill. He dismounted in the trees. It was cool and green, and the river gurgled happily. If he'd had the time, he'd like to have taken a proper bath and then a swim. He peered into the water and saw that there were a few nice-sized speckled trout, and he yearned to eat some fish. But instead, he trudged along the river toward the sawmill, making sure he did not step on a rattlesnake in the bushes or make any noise.

It was a sawmill all right, but it wasn't operating. Maybe it was Sunday or maybe the timber business was off at this time of year. At any rate, he saw the buckboard, the sorrel and the dapple so there wasn't any doubt that he had found Jessie. He sure hoped she was still alive.

With the bullwhip trailing behind and his arm poised to snap it forward, Black Snake moved stealthily forward until he reached a door to the building. The windows were so thickly coated with dirt, that he knew he wouldn't be able to see through them, so he did not even bother trying.

He could hear voices inside. The voices of men. Black Snake took up a couple of coils on his bullwhip for he did not want to enter the building with its rooms and maybe machinery and have his whip get caught in a doorway or something. He tiptoed foreward until he stood right up against a door and could hear the voices plainly. The pair of men were arguing.

"I say she's worth a goddamn fortune alive!" a deep voice said. "If we kill her right here and now, we'll kill the best chance we'll ever have of being rich."

"And I say, if we don't, they'll kill us when they realize we've betrayed them."

"Yeah, but how can they do that if we've already got the ransom and are sailing off to the Sandwich Islands?"

"You make it sound so easy! Ransoming people is tricky."

"Then let's get tricky," the deeper voice said. "She ain't even seen our faces. Hell, Colson and Pardee would do the same damn thing as us if they were at this end. I'm surprised they didn't think of it themselves."

"It's not them I'm worried about."

"You mean you're worried about D.C.?"

"Who the hell else? You know he's like a damn bulldog. He'd never quit until he had our hides nailed to a barn. We don't much want him on our tails."

"Piss on him! Like I said, we go to San Francisco, get a ransom and sail for the Islands. With the money they'll pay for this one, we can retire for the rest of our lives. Them island women will make us happy. Probably screw us to death."

The two men chuckled.

Black Snake looked around for a weapon, a piece of wood or an iron bar to hammer the pair across the skull with. He found a little flywheel about as big around as a cantaloupe and hefted it for balance. Between it, his pocket knife, which he now dug out of his pocket, and his bullwhip, he guessed he was as ready as he'd ever be to take the pair on.

Taking a deep breath and drawing back his throwing arm, he stepped into the doorway and saw Jessie and the two men. The larger one was a real giant, one whose size was so impressive that Black Snake just stared at the man. Why, he must have been seven feet tall. And ug—leeee!

The two looked at him, and when the smaller reacted by going for his gun first, Black Snake hurled the little flywheel and damned if it didn't catch the smaller, bearded fellow in the chest and knock the wind right out of him. The giant was slow, and had Black Snake remembered to bring his revolver, he could easily have outdrawn the man. But he didn't have his gun so he whipped his bullwhip forward and sent it winding around the giant's throat. The man gave a muffled roar. He grabbed the bullwhip and jerked Black Snake right off his feet and into his arms.

142

It was awful! One minute he was standing there admiring the work of his whip, the next minute he was under the strangling giant who now had his hands wrapped around Black Snake's gullet and was choking the life out of him.

It came down to who could go the longest without air, and since the giant had lost his about five seconds earlier, he started to turn purple first. Black Snake tried to buck the monster off his chest but it was hopeless. The animal was frothing and slavering all over him, and his eyes were bugging out as his fingers bit deeper and deeper into Black Snake's throat. Then, his tongue fell out and it was blue! And at the last minute, just when Black Snake thought he was a goner, a sure loser in the "how long can a man last without air" contest they were both playing, the giant collapsed on top of him.

The good part was that the massive hands released his windpipe. The bad part was that the giant was crushing him. Black Snake just managed to roll the man-mountain off him and to climb to his feet when the littler fella recovered enough to start crawling after the gun he'd dropped.

Jessie was blindfolded and still gagged, but she could still hear. She knew that someone or something was fighting. She staggered forward and tripped over the smaller kidnapper. Her head struck the floor, and she lost consciousness.

Black Snake beat the little man to his gun. Snatching it out of the man's grasp, he rolled and fired in one swift motion. His bullet went right through the man's skull.

Still unable to get his windpipe to open up, Black Snake rolled over onto his back and fought for air. He was in pain. Terrible pain! It would be almost a full hour before he could breath properly again. And sometime during his agonizing struggle, the giant died of asphyxiation.

When he could stand and breath normally again, Black

Snake picked Jessie up, carried her out of the sawmill and up the riverbank until he reached the horses. Then, he laid her down on a sandy strip and peeled off his clothes and waded into the Carson River. The water was warmed by sun and very much to his liking. He swam around a little and even floated on his back, enjoying the way the branches of the cottonwoods hung over the water from both banks and even met. Shafts of sunlight filtered through the canopy of leaves, and he studied the way their patterns stitched designs on the rippling surface of flowing water.

He heard a little splash, and then he whirled around cussing himself for not being more alert to danger.

Jessie swam out to his side. Black Snake's eyes widened a little as she passed through a shaft of light, and he saw the curving outline of her full and naked body.

"It's dangerous to go swimming with snakes in the water," he told her.

Jessie stood up for the water was only breast deep. "You once said you'd trade all your money to possess me."

"I spent my money to find you," he said.

"Hmmm. That's really something," she said, "given your obsession for money. I think such unselfishness should be rewarded."

He grinned. Moved up against her. She could feel his hard manhood bumping up against her belly. She reached down and took it in her hands, then spread her legs apart. "On the sandy beach, or right here and now?"

Black Snake chuckled. "Both. This first." His hands took her breasts and his thumbs begin to work her nipples until they contracted with desire. He bent down and sucked on one, then the other, and she moaned and began to rub his tool up and down between her legs. It felt wonderful in the cool river.

He straightened and reached around to grab her firm

144

buttocks. Then he rocked his hips forward and Jessie did the same. He seemed enormous as he drove up into her like a huge fish that began to wiggle in and out.

Jessie's head rolled back on her shoulders, and her long hair hung into the water. He took her fiercely, churning the water and lifting her up and down off the soft bed of the Carson River until the water grew muddy. And as their passion deepened, she raised herself on his manhood and then wrapped her long legs around his waist.

"Don't stop. Keep doing it just as long as you can, Black Snake."

"I will," he grunted hoarsely. "The only thing that's keepin' us from smokin' with fire down below is the water, Jessie."

She bit his shoulder, then teased his ear with her tongue, and it drove him like an engine, faster, deeper and harder. The way she liked it. And when he came inside of her, she cried out with delight and felt her own insides shudder and convulse on his driving root. A moment later, Black Snake collapsed in the churning water. He swore he would have drowned to death if she had not dragged him onto the sand and then grabbed his rod and pumped it up and down as if it were a water faucet handle.

Chapter 15

The Cheyenne were waiting, not only to starve or flush out Ki, Maggie and the beleaguered Circle Star cowboys, but also to attack the regularly scheduled Union Pacific train. Earlier this morning, they had dug themselves little depressions near the tracks and the charred remains of the Plum Creek Station. At noon, they had driven the Circle Star cattle and their horses behind some low hills to the north. At four o'clock, about thirty more warriors had arrived, and now they were of sufficient numbers to wipe out the train if they could take it by surprise.

"I guess the Army never got the message," Ed Wright grumbled. "When the train stops at that burnt-out station, those Indians will spring out of the ground like howling demons. They'll be all over the train before anyone can stop them."

Everyone looked to the samurai. When he said nothing, one of the cowboys said, "What can you do about it, Ki?"

"Why is it that Ki has to do everything!" Maggie Linker demanded. "He got us food. He's already been into their camp twice scattering horses and raising hell among the Indians. Isn't it time someone else did something besides hide here on this stinking island?"

The cowboys and their foreman were shamed because Maggie's words held ring of truth. So far, Ki had been the only one among them to do anything. "I'll go," Ed told them. "I'm in charge."

Ki touched the Circle Star foreman on the shoulder. "No offense," he said. "But you wouldn't get very far on foot. I'm the logical choice."

"It'll be suicide," Ed told him. "They've tightened up things so that not even a damned sand crab could sneak off this island until after dark. And from the looks of how things are going, the train is due any minute."

Ki had to agree. The Indians were hurrying to their hiding places, and he could see one with his ear to the iron rails. The man was gesturing with excitement, and it seemed clear to the samurai that the west-bound train was not far away.

"I'll wait until we hear or see the train, then I'll run for it," Ki decided. "With a little luck, I can alert them before they arrive."

"But what if the engineer just keeps on going and decides not to stop and help us?"

"That's another reason why I have to go," Ki said. "Because, if we just jumped up and started shooting, that's exactly what any intelligent engineer would do to protect his train and passengers. There's only five of us. There might be hundreds of passengers on board."

One of the cowboys said, "Well, it might be intelligent from his point of view, but it sure as hell stinks from where we sit!"

Ki could understand the cowboy's feelings very well. They'd been pinned down on this island for almost a week now, and they were about ready to go crazy, which was exactly what the Cheyenne were expecting. "I'll make sure they're warned in time to prepare a defense and also that they stop."

The cowboy nodded. "I didn't mean to lose my temper just now," he said. "There'll be women and children on that train, and I'd never do anything—even if it meant giving up all hope for ourselves—to put them in danger. I just want out of here."

Ki looked up at the sun, which was diving toward the western horizon. There was probably another hour of daylight left. The last of the Indians were taking cover, and the land seemed to have grown very, very still. But suddenly, far off to the east, he thought he heard a distant steam whistle blasting. Ki turned his head and said, "Listen!"

They all listened, and when the whistle blew again and again, they knew the train was coming. "There it is," Ki said, seeing the far off plume of black smoke puffing upward into a sky, which was just beginning to turn red with sunset.

Maggie touched his arm. "If you go now, they'll kill you for sure."

Ki tried to keep things light. "You've said that each time I've gone into their camp. When are you going to learn that I'm practically indestructible?"

His words had the desired effect, and she smiled and visibly relaxed. "Maybe you'll just outrun their bullets and arrows. Is that what a samurai does?"

"A samurai does whatever it takes to achieve his purpose. In this case, the Cheyenne have been forced to hide all their horses and can't run me down. I'll make it," he promised.

Ki prepared himself to go. The real danger would be in getting across the water and onto the shore. In the water, they could track him until he had to come out and then kill him before he could get away.

"Give me cover," he said, taking his bow and quiver and bursting out of the sand pit they had dug for themselves.

He hit the water in a low, reaching dive even before the first cry of warning was sounded by the Cheyenne who had been ordered to watch the besieged Texans. Ki stayed underwater as long as he could, and because he held his bow in one hand and his quiver of arrows in the other, he could not use his arms to pull himself forward. Instead, he relied upon the powerful kicking of his legs. He reached the riverbank without having to surface even once, and when he came up out of the water, his legs were churning and driving him up onto dry land.

The Cheyenne were caught by surprise, but they recovered quickly. While almost the entire force had been assigned to attack the approaching train when it ground to a halt, seven had remained near the Platte River to keep the Texan's pinned down so that they could not sound a warning.

Now, those seven came racing after Ki. Two of them were felled by bullets coming from the island, and the others came running after Ki as if their lives depended on his being overtaken and slain.

But the samurai was more than a match for their speed and endurance. The Cheyenne were the finest horsemen of the Plains, but they disdained walking almost as much as a Texas cowboy. Because of that, they quickly fell behind, and when it was obvious that they could not overtake the samurai, then used bows and rifles to try and bring him down before he could reach the approaching train.

The arrows fell short, but one bullet struck Ki in the upper leg and sent him tumbling to the grass. With a cry of joy, the Indians took heart and rushed forward. Ki did not bother to pull the arrow from his leg. He struggled to his feet, breaking the shaft off inches from his flesh and tried to run. But after a dozen faltering strides, it was obvious that he was not going to make it. The Cheyenne were closing fast. Ki spun around, and even though his leg was growing numb and useless, there was nothing wrong with his arms, his shoulders and his extraordinary reactions.

He selected the "death song" arrow that was tipped with a small ceramic bulb just behind the point. The bulb had a tiny hole through it so that as the arrow streaked toward its target, it spun and the air-hole screamed like a banshee. Now, Ki fired the arrow, and it began its screaming flight. The Cheyenne saw the arrow coming at them. Its unnatural shriek drove fear into their hearts. So not only did it kill the fleetest Indian, but it stopped those behind him in their tracks and filled them with dread.

Ki turned and ran on. The Indians hesitated a moment and then realized that Ed Wright, Maggie and the two cowboys had decided to break for the train rather than to wait any longer. In a swift, violent confrontation, the Cheyenne and the Texans fired round after round, and when the last of the Indians fell, only Ed and Maggie were alive to race after the hobbling samurai. They caught him, and he threw his arms across their shoulders as they struggled toward the approaching train.

By now, the rest of the war party had realized what had happened and that there was no longer the possibility of surprising the engineer. Outraged that their plans had gone awry, they were determined to overtake and scalp their quarry.

Ed looked over his shoulder. "We'll never make it," he said. "It looks like there are at least fifty of them."

"Don't talk!" Ki gritted. Keep running and, if they get within range, drop me and go on!"

"The hell with that!" Maggie cried, already gasping for breath.

If it had not been for the fact that the engineer saw them coming and after initially slowing down to stop, now was accelerating, Ki knew they'd be overtaken by the Indians.

"We've got to get up into the coal car," Ki shouted. "If we wait any longer, they'll be on top of us."

Maggie nodded, but she didn't look as if she could make it. Ed wright wasn't a young man, and he was also pale and running out of reserves. But Ki forced himself to ignore his leg and, as they neared the huge locomotive, he could see the engineer's face very distinctly. The man looked scared out of his wits. He kept blasting the steam whistle as if he thought it might actually scare off the charging Indians.

When they finally reached the tracks, the train's engine was almost on top of them. It looked huge and menacing. Smoke was pouring out its stack and it was picking up speed. Ki was not sure that they would be able to grab onto the coal tender and swing aboard.

"Stand steady!" Ki shouted as arrows and bullets began to reach for them, "forget about the Indians!"

Ki slung his bow and quiver over his shoulder and positioned the Circle Star foreman and Maggie. "Jump for the platform that joins the two. Do it NOW!"

Ki practically threw the young woman upward, and she sprawled into the coal tender. Ed jumped, but there was no spring to his legs. He barely managed to grab a bar handle, and then he was jerked out of his tracks as the train roared westward. He hung along its side. Then, Maggie reached out for him and pulled him on board. Ki thought he heard her scream out his name, but he was already throwing himself at the platform just behind the coal tender.

It would have been very easy if it were not for his bad

leg. As it was, he had to push off on one leg, and he very nearly fell under the iron wheels. For a moment, his lower body dragged along the rocky tracks and struck each and every railroad tie. Then, as another arrow cut his cheek before burying itself in the wood siding of the first passenger car, Ki pulled himself up to safety. He hopped up the iron railing attached the back of the coal tender and dropped over its side, to tumble down a mountain of coal and come to a halt beside Maggie and Ed who were crouched down and firing out at the Indians with pistols.

"You made it!" Maggie cried with happiness. "You made it."

He was covered with coal dust, but then, so were they. Ki sleeved it out of his eyes and grinned. He dared to stick his head out to see their train roaring through the burned out Plum Creek Station. Up in the cab of the engine, the engineer was flat on the floor. He'd wisely tied the throttle down and hit the deck as a hail of arrows and bullets crashed and pelted the locomotive and passenger cars.

Ki leaned out from the coal tender and saw the Indians disappear. Even had they been mounted on their ponies, they'd not have been able to match the train's current speed.

The engineer peered around and gave them a very tentative smile. "I'm sorry I couldn't stop and make things easier for you. But as you can see, we've got a lot of passengers and they're my responsibility. I did what I had to do."

Ki nodded. "No apology necessary. You did the right thing."

The man stood up, now that the danger was past. "I never even saw the herd of Texas cattle we were supposed to load."

"The Indians got them."

152

"That's a damn shame," the engineer said. "Thievin' redskins. Why, fifteen hundred head will feed them through one, maybe even two winters. I hate to see that. The only way to get rid of them is to starve them out."

Ki said nothing. He guessed he should have been grateful that he, Maggie and Ed were still alive, but he could not forget that a lot of good Circle Star cowboys had died at Plum Creek on the Platte River. Died trying to save their herd of Texas cattle. Died for nothing because the herd was now lost.

"There's nothing more any of us could do to get the cowboys or the herd back," Ed told him, reading his dark thoughts. "Jessie gave us orders to desert the cattle if it came down to them or the men."

Ki looked up at the Circle Star foreman. "We lost both," he said. "That's what bothers me the most. I'm not used to failure. No samurai is."

"We didn't fail completely," Maggie said. "Who knows how many passengers on this train are alive because we gave them the alarm? You did more than any man could have done."

Ki looked down at the arrowhead still imbedded in his thigh. He unsheathed his *tanto* knife and before anyone could protest, he made two quick cuts and pulled the wicked arrowhead free.

Maggie tore her dress and quickly bandaged the wound as Ki reflected on what the engineer had just said about starving the Indians out of existence. He did not agree with that philosophy, and he told Maggie so. "We're killing off their buffalo by the tens of thousands. I guess fifteen hundred Texas cattle aren't so much a price to pay them in return. Those cattle will be eaten by starving Indian women and children. I guess it's only fair."

He hugged Maggie who had listened to his words and

finally showed tears. Tears of relief, tears of gratitude and happiness. "Let's get you to a passenger car," she said. There's bound to be a doctor on this train somewhere. I don't want to deliver you to Miss Starbuck in such bad condition that you can't even stand on your feet."

Yes, Ki thought, it is time to go help Jessie. That is what I have vowed to do as a true samurai. It is my mission to protect *her*, not a herd of cattle, from all enemies. And this I will do!

Chapter 16

It was almost midnight, and time for the graveyard shift to go down into the bowels of the Bonanza Unlimited. Jessie and Black Snake were posing as miners as the shift plodded past a half-drunken guard. The guard smiled and was unusually jolly. He could not figure out why anyone would forget an entire bottle of whiskey and leave it where a man like himself could find it this cold Comstock night, but it was his good fortune.

Because the darkness was illuminated by only a few kerosene lanterns, Jessie was not greatly worried that anyone would recognize her. Like all the others, she was dressed in dirty work clothes and a heavy canvas coat. She wore a slouch hat pulled low over her eyes, and her hair was braided and hidden by her collar. Half of the crew were foreigners, and many of those around her smelled heavily of whiskey. There was little conversation, and as they filed into the huge tin mining works and stood in line awaiting the cage that would drop them down into the mine, Jessie could feel her stomach churn with anxiety. She was slightly claustrophobic and had never been underground as deep as they were about to go now.

Black Snake didn't like the idea of going underground

155

any better than she did. He was very quiet, and she knew that he had his whip wrapped around his waist and well hidden under his coat. If there was any trouble, Jessie was prepared for it this time. She had her derringer and her Colt pistol, and she'd not hesitate to use them.

She whispered to Black Snake. "Cheer up, this could be a real adventure."

He leaned very close to her. "It could also be our funerals. I always figured the deepest I'd go was six feet under."

Enveloped in a cloud of steam, the cage slammed to the surface with such violence that Jessie staggered back into a miner who grunted and shoved her forward. "Stay offa my goddamn toes!"

"Sorry," she said in her deepest voice as she watched the evening shift unload from the cage platform. They were sweating heavily and looked totally exhausted by their underground labors.

"How hot is it at the sixteenth!" a man called.

"Only a 132 degrees tonight. Don't worry, we used up all your ice."

"Sonofabitch."

Jessie shook her head. She had never faced temperatures like that before. If the cage stopped at many levels on the way to its 1600 foot base, she intended to see that she and Black Snake got off at the thousand foot station. There, the temperature was supposed to be an even hundred degrees. It got that hot in Texas, so Jessie figured she could stand it for a while.

As soon as the cage emptied, twenty men on the graveyard shift stumbled foreward to climb into the cage for the descent. The cage was little more than an iron platform with single welded pipe around its perimeter. About eight feet square, it dangled from a braided wire cable held by a huge winding spool. At the controls of a steam engine, an engineer suddenly threw a lever forward, and the cage vanished as the wire cable flew off the winding wheel so fast that it blurred as it disappeared down the shaft.

Black Snake turned around and tried to leave. Jessie caught his arm and whispered in his ear the only words that would keep him by her side. "A thousand dollars if we discover the reason behind my friend's being murdered."

The man froze. He considered the offer very, very carefully. Cussing his own greed, Black Snake returned to his place in the line. Their wait was brief. It seemed to take no time at all before the engineer threw another lever and the cable stopped reeling out. Two, maybe three minutes passed and the man at the controls received a signal from far down below by means of a cable and a series of bell rings. The man yanked the lever back and the winding wheel began to protest, then gather speed. The steam engine whined in protest as the cage and the second half of the graveyard shift was jerked up from the bottom of the shaft and brought to the surface.

Once more, Jessie saw the weary, dirt-covered faces of the miners brought to the surface. Only this time, she and Black Snake were being shoved forward in line and onto the cage. Jessie squeezed as near to the center as possible. She could feel the cage bounce up and down as if it were resting on springs. It made her feel hollow in the stomach, and the steam that lifted all around them filled her with dread. When she looked at Black Snake for support, she found none: he was already sweating with fear and his eyes were closed. Jessie could feel hot air lifting out of the hole below them. She closed her eyes too and then the floor seemed to drop out from under their feet.

It was the most horrible feeling imaginable. It was like falling forever as the cage dropped sixteen hundred feet into hell. Jessie's eyes popped open, and she bit her lips until they bled to keep from screaming in terror. Even though the noise of the engine, the twisting cage and cable were so loud that no one could possibly have heard her. She saw blips of light, and it was only after they had passed the fourteen hundred foot level and began to slow their descent that she realized that the blips of light had been huge underground caverns where miners worked at each hundred foot level.

When the cage jerked to a halt, it seemed to yo-yo up and down on its thin, wire thread. Jessie wanted to vomit, and the heat seemed unbearable. If she hadn't have been packed in so tightly, she'd have collapsed. Black Snake looked pasty too in the lamplight. Somehow, they staggered off the cage into the big station.

The men plodded over to a wall where tools were stacked. "So much for our plan to stop at the thousand foot level," Black Snake said as he craned his head back and looked up at the ingenious square-set timbering invented by the great German mining engineer, Phillip Deidesheimer. Jessie followed his gaze because the sight was truly amazing. The entire station was supported by huge, interlocking timbers that formed sets of squares which were all buttressed by more timbers. Jessie knew that the Comstock was plagued by clay that expanded when it was uncovered. Expanding clay collapsed traditional methods of shoring up mines and only the square-set design had proven itself in these hellish conditions and at these depths.

"Hey, you two, let's go!" a man yelled. Jessie guessed he was probably the mining shift boss or supervisor.

"Uh-oh," Jessie said, watching as the miners stripped off their coats and then their shirts until their bare chests already glistened in the punishing heat. "It would appear I've got a problem."

"Damn right you do," Black Snake said, managing to smile. "Two *big* problems!"

"Stop grinning and figure out some way to cause a distraction while I go for that tunnel running north!"

Black Snake realized she was dead serious. He pulled off his coat and walked quickly over toward the tools. Knocking one miner aside, he grabbed a pick from another and said, "This is my special pick! Find one of your own!"

The two startled miners could not believe him. One of them said, "A pick is a pick, you dumb sonofabitch!"

In reply, Black Snake dropped the pick on the man's boot. When he howled with pain, the second man attacked, and suddenly, there was a full-scale donnybrook.

Black Snake was taking a whale of a beating. Fortunately, the shift supervisor was putting an end to the fight. Jessie removed her coat, but she was still perspiring heavily. Black Snake, she promised, if this works, you'll be rewarded.

Jessie pulled one of the kerosene lamps from the wall to guide her. She had a compass and now she studied it to make sure of her direction. The tunnel she headed for was directly north toward the Crossfire Mining claim. Maybe she was in luck.

When she reached the tunnel, she ducked into it and began counting her steps. Whenever the tunnel turned, she noted its direction and kept moving forward, always counting, always writing down both direction and distance. It was hot and dangerous work: there were holes and treacherous inclines all along the tunnel leading down into even greater depths. In fact, if you did not stay right between the little ore-cart tracks, you would probably fall and never be found.

Jessie tried not to think too much about the heat and the many pitfalls as she cautiously moved forward. Suddenly, she turned a corner and found herself standing right in the middle of a huge mining station complete with its own cage and shaft. A shift of miners was just now unloading and she was caught flat-footed and in plain sight.

Dazed by the heat and dazzled by the sudden bright light, Jessie was momentarily blinded as the thought flashed across her mind, this is the Crossfire Mine! It could be no other, and this proved the two mines were secretly connected.

"Hey!" a man shouted. "What the hell . . . it's a woman! Let's get her!

Without her coat, Jessie's figure was unmistakably female. She saw a wall of men running for her, and she knew that she was in deep trouble. She whirled around and took off running. In her haste, the lantern in her hand was extinguished, and suddenly, she was running blind.

The worse thing possible happened. Her foot struck one of the rails and she was thrown off balance. Windmilling her arms and fighting to stay within the tracks, she struck a timber and then dropped. A scream filled her throat. The hole she was tumbling down was as black as the center of earth. Jessie was certain she was going to die. She fell until she struck a pool of hot, stinking water. It broke her fall and saved her life. Jessie clawed at the sides of the hole and gasped for breath. The hole was filled with steam.

"Help!" she cried. "Help!"

Pebbles rained down on her. She heard voices high above her and then the unmistakable pop of a bullwhip followed by gunfire. Heart-stopping moments later, she was suddenly greeted by more cascading pebbles. And then, to her horror, she heard a grunt and the sound of a falling body. Jessie hugged the slippery side of the hole and said a quick prayer that the fall would not kill her or Black Snake.

He hit the water with a tremendous splash, and Jessie spun around and groped for him in the darkness. She found his boots, then his belt and grabbing his head, she pulled his face out of the water and hugged him tightly. "Damn you!" she screamed up at the men above.

Laughter drifted down to her and the circle of lamplight light vanished. Jessie groped for Black Snake's pulse. She found it and closed her eyes in the absolute darkness. Maybe it would have been better if he had broken his neck and hers too for there was no hope of escape from this steaming hell hole. None at all.

Mike Colson and Dirk Pardee heard the news almost immediately. Their mine offices were connected by an underground telegraph line, just as Jessie had suspected. Colson, the younger of the pair was first to arrive at the sixteen hundred foot level, but Pardee was there just a few minutes later.

Colson raised his lantern over the deep pit and said, "Are you sure she's still alive?"

The shift foreman nodded his head. "She was ten minutes ago 'cause she yelled, 'damn you' right after we threw the big guy with the bullwhip in after her."

Pardee shook his head. "How deep is it to the bottom?"

"About twenty-five or thirty feet. It was just another probe for the vein we been following. We gave it up last month when it started to fill with water. I decided to use it as just another fill hole."

"Go ahead and do it then," Pardee said. "Bury them."

But Colson shook his head. "I don't know," he said. "I did some checking up on that woman after she left my office. She's worth millions of dollars. Ought to be some way to profit on it."

"There isn't!" Pardee snapped. "I say we bury them up and be done with it."

The mine shift foreman shook his head. "I hate to do that. I mean, if they'd have died in the fall, it wouldn't be so bad. But to bury a woman alive. . . ."

Colson felt the same way, though he did not want to say it outright and reveal his squeamishness. "Maybe we should get her out of there. Leave the man but get the woman and see if we can think of something better."

Pardee was sweating profusely. "I tell you, if we get greedy and try to ransom her, we'll lose everything!"

"Yeah," Colson argued, "but think about this. If she suspected that the Bonanza Unlimited and the Crossfire Mine are working together, who else might be suspicious? And you know what will happen if that information got out before we can take care of business?"

Pardee knew full well. By joining the two mines in secret, they could transfer tons of gold and silver ore back and forth and thus control the weekly production figures. It was those tonnages that directly determined the value of both the Crossfire and Bonanza stock selling all over the world. By manipulating those two stock values, Colson, Pardee and a few others could and did make enormous stock market profits each week based on the fluctuating stock values of the Crossfire and Bonanza mines. And the stock market was where the real fortunes were being won.

But there were great risks. Sarah Sawyer, working in the Crossfire offices, had figured out the game, and so she'd been eliminated within hours. Her husband, Grant, had been immediately suspicious, and when he'd come down into the mine, he'd been eliminated too. And now, there was Jessica Starbuck and some big, bull-whipping sonofabitch, and Pardee hoped they were the last.

"Let's leave them be," he said. "They can't last but a

day or two. When this blows over, we'll get a fresh crew in here to fill up the hole. They'll never be found."

Colson nodded. "Terrible way to go."

"She should have kept her pretty nose out of our business," Pardee said. "Let's get out of here."

He turned to the mine foreman, noting how the sweat streaming down his face made him look as if he'd just climbed out of a hot bath. "I want you and each mine foreman on each shift to keep this tunnel off limits."

"We'll do it," the man said. "I'll wall up both ends of this connecting tunnel."

Pardee was satisfied. "I'll fill D.C. in on what happened to her."

"He won't be happy."

"The hell with him," Pardee said. "He takes care of business up on top, but down here, we're in charge. Sometimes, he forgets that."

"Just as long as you're the one that reminds him and not me," Colson said.

The two mine superintendents split up and each headed in the opposite direction toward their own shafts. Mining and murder were dirty business. But when millions of dollars stood to be won or lost, a man could buy a lot of soap to wash away dirt or blood.

Chapter 17

Ki, Maggie and Ed Wright arrived in Reno by train. Ki was anxious to find Jessie and protect her from any harm. He'd even allowed himself to hope that she might be waiting at the Reno train station, but that had not been the case. "Maggie, I want you to stay here in Reno while I go to the Comstock."

"Please, can't I go with you?"

"I'm afraid that would not be in anyone's best interests," Ki said. His leg wound was painful, and it decreased his mobility. But Ki was determined not to allow the pain of an arrow wound to distract him from his purpose.

She saw that his mind was made up. "Only if you promise to come back and say goodbye to me before you return to Texas."

Ki nodded. "On that, I give you my word."

Maggie knew that she was going to lose Ki very soon. There was no sense in trying to hang onto him, no sense even in hoping that the samurai would ever give up his vow of always protecting Jessica Starbuck. "All right then."

Ki and Ed Wright hurried to the stage station only to

learn that the next stage heading south would not leave for almost three hours.

"Too long," Ki said.

"I agree. Let's find a livery and rent horses."

Twenty minutes later, they were galloping south, and by noon, they'd found the three Circle Star cowboys and the herd of Texas cattle. "Has Jessie been down from Virginia City yet!" Ki asked.

"Afraid not." Joe looked worried. "She told us to graze the herd south and wait for her. She wanted these cattle in good condition. That's what we're doing now."

Ed Wright nodded. His professional eye judged the cattle and he was satisfied with what he saw. The Circle Star cattle were fattening up in a hurry on the rich valley grass.

"Did you send the rest of the boys on back to the ranch?" Joe asked. "We sure are lookin' forward to seeing Texas again."

A shadow passed across Ed's lined face. A face that reflected how hard he had taken the loss of his herd and Circle Star cowboys back on the Nebraska plains. "I'm afraid we were hit by Indians pretty hard. The others are dead. The Cheyenne got the rest of the herd. We were lucky to get out of Plum Creek Station with our lives."

Joe and his two cowboys looked away quickly, and then each one wandered off alone to consider the loss of their friends.

Ki switched his saddle from one of the rented horses to a fresh Circle Star cowpony. "I'm going up to Virginia City and find her. You stay here with the herd."

"I'll give you twenty-four hours," Ed told him. "If you aren't back with Jessie by then, we'll leave one man here and three of us will come up and tear the Comstock apart if that's what it's going to take to get to the bottom of things."

"All right," Ki said, knowing that argument was futile. Ed considered himself almost like Jessie's father. He'd be worried half-sick until he saw her again. "Twenty-four hours."

Ki rode due east from the big valley located between Reno and Carson City. He climbed over the barren hills through the already abandoned mining town of Jumbo and entered Virginia City by circling around Sun Mountain. The first place he tied his horse was in front of the Sheriff's Office.

Deputy Tom Cutter greeted him cooly. "I haven't seen Miss Starbuck since she arrived, and I told her what I knew of the Sawyer case. The coroner ruled that Mrs. Sawyer died of natural causes and her husband fell down the Bonanza Unlimited's mine shaft."

Ki shook his head. "Jessie didn't believe that, did she?"

"I don't think so," Cutter said. "She showed me a telegram from Mr. Sawyer that indicated he thought his wife had been murdered and his own life was in danger. I told her what I knew and suggested she speak to Dan DeQuille or even the coroner himself, Doctor Butterman."

"And did she?"

"I don't know. I'm acting sheriff right now. This is a rough mining town. People getting mugged, murdered and maimed every day and night. I just don't have time to investigate much of anything. I've asked for more money to hire more staff. I ought to be made sheriff and get a sheriff's pay while I'm holding things down, but I guess even that is too much for the town council to handle. Everyone is getting rich around here, and I'm the one that's supposed to keep law and order. Why, if—"

Ki had no time to listen to the complaints of this man. They were probably justified, but it was not his concern

—Jessie was the only thing that counted. "Thanks for your help."

The deputy followed him to the door. "If you ask me, I'd say she left the Comstock after she decided that Sawyer's telegram was in error. I haven't seen her since that first day."

"She probably went to ask questions at the Bonanza and the Crossfire mines," Ki said. "I guess that's where I'll start too."

"Be a waste of time to do that. They've guards posted at both mines. You'll never set foot on the property. If I was you, I'd check the Occidental Hotel. That's where she was staying. As for the Sawyers, I'd tell you the same things I told Miss Starbuck. Talk to Dan DeQuille or Doc Butterman. They'll tell you that both the husband and wife died without any suspicious circumstances."

"Anytime two relatively young and healthy people die within a short time of each other, the circumstances ought to be considered highly suspicious," Ki said as he headed for the door. "What I intend to do is find Miss Starbuck."

Cutter threw up his hands in a gesture of resignation. "Be my guest. But I'm telling you, she's gone. I hope she left you a message at the hotel, but if she didn't, you might find she's in San Francisco by now."

Ki didn't believe that for a single minute. But he would not waste his breath to tell this man so. Standing on the boardwalk, he turned and said, "Excuse me, but I have just one more question. At which livery did she board her horse?"

"Why . . . what horse? She told me she came to Reno by train."

"She did. But she also brought fifteen hundred cattle, three cowboys and four horses. One of them was her own personal favorite, a palomino named Sun. She'd never leave him behind. Now, which stable would be recommended as being this city's finest?"

Cutter was at a loss for words. "I don't know. They're all about the same."

Ki turned away. There could not be more than four or five. If he got lucky, he'd find the right one first, if not, it might take an hour of painful limping, but by then he'd have his answer.

Ki stopped by the Occidental Hotel. The desk clerk was old, wizened and very suspicious until Ki showed the man a Circle Star design he carried and convinced the man that he was employed by Jessie and the Circle Star ranch. "She'll be expecting me."

"I haven't seen her since early yesterday morning," he said, checking the pigeon hole behind his hotel counter. "I'm sorry. No messages for you."

"Any idea where she was going?"

"No."

"I want to see her room."

"I'm afraid that is out of the question."

Ki could have easily rendered the man unconscious and then gotten the hotel key, but he decided not to use force. "Do you know where she might have boarded her horse?"

"Yes I do. George Austin's Stable down at the end of "C" Street is our finest. That's where she took him."

"Thank you."

Ki hurried out of the hotel. He mounted his horse and rode toward the end of the street. When he saw the stable, he tied his horse up and walked into the barn.

"Anyone here!"

No one answered, and yet he heard a horse's hooves drumming somewhere behind the barn. Ki raced through the barn and out the back door just in time to see a man leading Sun away as fast as he could. The long-legged palomino was trotting along behind and Ki shouted, "Stop right there!"

The man jumped behind Sun, drew his gun and opened fire.

Ki was caught without cover. He wanted answers, not blood, but with the palomino jumping around, there was no choice but to aim for the man's forehead. His *shuriken* blade spun forward and struck the man squarely between the eyes.

The gunman screamed, his Colt dropped to the earth, and Sun ran away in fright with Ki limping after him. The horse-thief was dead. There was no question about that. The real question was, why was he trying to steal the palomino in broad daylight?

Ki caught the palomino at the end of "D" street where it took a fancy to a pretty sorrel mare. He led Jessie's horse back to the livery and, by now, there was a big crowd around the dead horse-thief.

"That's him!" someone shouted. "He's the one that threw that shiny little blade and killed Jack! He's the one!"

Deputy Cutter drew his gun. The samurai knew there was no chance of escape without risking a gunfight in which several spectators would likely be killed, possibly even women and children among the crowd. With great reluctance, Ki surrendered.

"I hope you have a good reason for arresting me," Ki said. "It shouldn't be hard to prove that this palomino belongs to Miss Jessica Starbuck and that it was being stolen."

Deputy Cutter handcuffed the samurai. "If that's the case, you'll be released as soon as we can find George Austin."

"He's dead!" someone yelled as they came rushing out

of the barn. "Still bleeding with a knife in his back! A *Chinese* knife."

Cutter looked right through Ki. "Your knife?"

"No," Ki said. "If you will reach under my shirt, you'll find my knife."

The deputy removed Ki's *tanto* blade in its laqurered sheath. "A lot of Chinamen carry two, even three knives."

"I'm not Chinese," Ki said, trying to control his anger. "I'm Japanese and white."

But the deputy shook his head. "I don't know," he said. "You were in that barn, weren't you?"

"Yes, but—"

"It doesn't look good for you," Cutter said. "It doesn't look good at all."

Ki studied the faces of the crowd. He saw real hostility. Maybe, like most people, they just saw that his eyes were almond shaped and his skin was golden instead of white. That he wore sandals instead of boots and that he preferred Oriental to Western weapons. Sometimes, just being different was enough to make a man guilty until proven innocent.

Chapter 18

The sides and floor of the Virginia City jail was made of solid rock and mortar. The ceiling was at least eighteen feet overhead and constructed of heavy legs. Even for a samurai, it was going to take some time to escape. The jail contained three cells located in the rear of the building that were separated from the sheriff's office by a thick wall. In effect, even if a man escaped his cell, he might find himself unable to reach the front entry.

Ki sat on a small bunk and considered his next moves. Once he did escape, where would he start looking for Jessie? It was clear that she was still on the Comstock or else she would have taken Sun. He also continued to puzzle over the question of why someone had been trying to steal Jessie's horse in broad daylight and why the liveryman had been murdered only a few moments before Ki arrived.

Ki heard Cutter and another man arguing, then the hall door opened and a tall, stern appearing man with ink-stained hands appeared.

"Ten minutes," Cutter said angrily. "That's all you get with him."

The man closed the door behind his back and looked at

the samurai. "So you," he said in a deep, gravelly voice, "are the famed Starbuck samurai."

"Who are you?"

"Dan DeQuille. Reporter with *The Territorial Enterprise*. Would you mind answering a few questions?"

"Yes, I would. Unless you care to answer a few of my questions first."

DeQuille frowned. "That is not the way it is supposed to work," he said. "However, since you are without a doubt a real samurai who managed to kill a man today with a silver star blade instead of the usual boring gun or knife, I'd be willing to cooperate if the questions are brief."

"They are," Ki said. Very quickly, he told DeQuille about Deputy Cutter's surprise that Jessie had ridden a horse up to Virginia City. "He tried to convince me that Jessie had left the Comstock. And when he learned I was going to check the stables, he must have sent that man to steal her horse."

"And murder poor George Austin?" DeQuille shook his head. "Tom Cutter is a hard man and quite ambitious. But not *that* ambitious."

Ki shrugged his shoulders. "How else can you explain such a coincidence? He was the only one who knew I was going to the Occidental and then the stables. And after I killed an obvious horse thief, he sure was eager to put me in jail. It had to be the Deputy. Who's the sheriff?"

"It's Tom's cousin, Dick Cutter. He's been laid up with a bullet."

"And his cousin has taken his place?"

"That's right." DeQuille frowned. "Dick is best friends with Doctor Butterman. I've had the feeling they were very much in league with some sort of Comstock business."

"Then that's it," Ki said. "The deputy is just the front. Probably the enforcer. I'll bet he's fast with that gun."

"Oh, you can be sure of that," DeQuille said. "And I have heard rumors that his cousin has been heavily involved in the mining stocks. Of course, on a sheriff's pay, that would be impossible so I discounted that kind of talk as nothing but idle gossip."

"It's not gossip. They're all related in this somehow, and I intend to find out after we find Miss Starbuck."

"Do you have any idea where she might be?" the reporter asked.

"No," Ki said, gripping the bars. "Mr. DeQuille you apparently know something about me and Miss Starbuck."

"I do."

"Then I need your help in finding Jessie."

"In return for?"

"Name your price," Ki said.

"Very well, in addition to this whole intriguing business of kidnapping and our deputy being in cahoots with a murder, I want the complete story of the skills of *ninja* and a samurai. I have heard accounts about them, and our readers would be fascinated to learn about them as well. I also wish to have revealed for my readers the entire account concerning Miss Starbuck's involvement on the Comstock. She came to visit me when she first arrived, and I'm afraid I was under a newspaper deadline and did not really pursue her story as well as I should have. I regret that oversight. I'd like to make up for it. So do we have a deal, Mr. Ki?"

Ki had never consented to an interview, but now he realized he had no choice. Besides, this man could have asked for money or special favors from Jessie, but he'd only asked for a fascinating news story. The request said a great deal about DeQuille's professional integrity. "I agree to tell you everything I can about *ninjutsu*, 'the art of the invisible assassin,' though I doubt that few of your readers would believe what I say."

DeQuille was obviously delighted. He stuck his hand through the bars and said, "I'll believe, and so will anyone else who saw that star blade embedded in that horse thief's forehead. Now, how can I help?"

"Begin by telling me everything you know about the Sawyers and the circumstances of their deaths."

DeQuille quickly told Ki everything he knew. He finished his narrative by saying, "Now what, samurai?"

"Get the deputy out of the office for just a few minutes on some pretense so that I can escape without killing the man. Then, meet me outside the Bonanza Unlimited."

"But why! They won't let me set foot in that mine."

"Jessica Starbuck is on the Comstock," Ki said. "The Sawyers were killed working for the Bonanza and the Crossfire mines. They are the obvious places to start looking."

"Perhaps so, but—"

"Mr. DeQuille," Ki said. "You're probably the most respected authority on the Comstock. You've already told me that those two mines are adjacent to each other. Now, assuming they are both responsible for the deaths of Sarah and Grant Sawyer, what would they have to gain in common?"

DeQuille was happy to expound. "Merely by shuttling ore back and forth, they could play one's rising stock against the other's falling stock to their own advantage. It's been done before, but never with two operations that size."

Ki thought about it. "It is the most logical explanation," he said. "I just hope we aren't too late to save Jessie. And if we are, heads will roll before this day is over."

DeQuille took a deep breath. "Your assumptions and conclusions concerning our sheriff and his deputy, in addition to Doctor Butterman and both the Bonanza and Cross-fire mines are chilling. The murders—if they were indeed murders—of the Sawyer couple are tragic. I pray you're wrong."

"Help me to escape by getting Cutter off on a ruse of some sort, then meet me at once at the Bonanza Unlimited Mine."

DeQuille stroked his beard and nodded. "Yes," he said. "I will most certainly do that."

When the door closed behind DeQuille, Ki removed a thin wire from his jacket. A *ninja* could use the wire to strangle, catch fish, or even replace his bow-string in an emergency. Now, Ki inserted the wire into the heavy cell lock. Kneeling down and pressing his ear to the lock, he concentrated using both his finely tuned sense of hearing and touch to move the tumblers. When the lock clicked, he pushed the cell door open.

Ki re-inserted the wire into his tunic, and then he stepped to the hall door and listened. He was just in time to hear the front door close. DeQuille had accomplished his mission, and when Ki stepped into the sheriff's office, it was empty. A moment later, he had gathered his collection of weapons and was gliding out the doorway and down between buildings toward "D" Street. There was little doubt in Ki's mind that Deputy Cutter was part of some evil conspiracy. Later on he might have to kill the man, but to do so now would create an entire set of new problems.

"Tell them that I have permission to go down into the mines," Ki said to the newspaper reporter.

"For what purpose?"

"I don't know. You're the expert. The man whom every-one on the Comstock has to trust. The only man in Virginia City who could start or stop a gold or silver crash with nothing but a misplaced rumor. Say anything."

DeQuille dusted off his black frocked coat and straightened his tie. He was well over six feet tall and quite imposing as he marched up to the guards while Ki stood back and watched. Ki saw the reporter gesture back toward him, then point down into the mine. He saw the guards look questioningly and then go into a sort of huddle. A moment later, one of the guards took off for the mine offices.

Ki knew that DeQuille and been unable to convince the guards that they had arrived on some legitimate errand. He also knew that he could not allow the guards to reach the big tin building and raise the alarm. Ki jumped forward and used the hard muscles along the edge of his tensed hand to deliver a *tegatana* blow to the base of one guard's neck. Unfortunately, the second guard happened to glance around and see his companion fall. He took off running.

Ki had no wish to kill the man but neither could he expect to overtake him before he reached the mine superintendent's office given his own wounded leg. So he did the only thing he could do. He reached for the *surushin* wrapped around his waist. The *surushin* was six foot length of rope with leather-covered steel balls at each end. With a quick overhead throwing motion, Ki sent the *surushin* spinning after the guard. It overtook him with a whirring sound and wrapped itself around his legs and brought him crashing to the earth.

The man's breath was knocked from his lungs, and before he could recover enough to shout for help, Ki was on him and administering *atemi*. He pulled the guard off into the brush where he would not be seen and motioned for DeQuille to do the same.

"So much for trust," DeQuille said cryptically as they headed toward the shaft.

The hoisting wheel operator did not question their desire

to descend into the mine, only the particular level they wanted to visit. "It's like hell down there," DeQuille said. "So let's get the worst over first and start at the bottom."

Ki nodded. It seemed obvious to him that, if you were going to get rid of someone, you'd bury or imprison them at the bottom of the mine rather than at the top or the middle. Ki stepped onto the bouncy cage and grabbed the center pole. He could feel the steam rising up between his legs, and he closed his eyes as the cage dropped out from under him and his stomach lifted up to fill his mouth.

Jessie did not think she and Black Snake could last more than a few hours. Escape was impossible, and yet they had never given up trying. She had clawed at the sides of the pit until her fingernails were bloodied, and still the smooth, wet clay would offer no handhold. The clay was too soft and broke away under their weight. She had even climbed onto Black Snake's shoulders and flailed his whip in the desperate hope that it's popper might somehow snag or catch on some overhead protrusion, enabling her to climb up to safety. But the pit was so narrow and the whip so long that she had been unable to swing it effectively.

The hot water had sapped their strength and made it hard to breath. Jessie had lost track of time. Now, the easiest thing in the world would have been to just sink down in to the water and wait until the mind drifted into unconsciousness.

But neither of them were quitters, and so they stood side by side in the waist-high water and kept trying to think of some means of escape. Jessie hugged Black Snake and said, "It looks a little grim for us, doesn't it?"

"Worse than grim," he said. "It looks damn near fatal to me. I'd say, if you got any good prayers, use 'em now."

"I have," Jessie said.

"Me too. But if we ever get out of—"

"Shhhh! Listen! Jessie whispered.

They both heard the clanking sound of an ore cart being rolled along the tracks above. Jessie stiffened when the cart seemed to stop right overhead. She heard the scrape of a shovel against rock and metal, and then she sensed rather than saw the shower of rock and gravel that was falling down on them. Black Snake must have sensed it too because he shoved Jessie against the clay wall and covered her with his body. Jessie felt smothered and nearly sick with panic. Most of the rocks missed them but a few struck Black Snake, and she felt his powerful body jerk with their impact.

"Stop it!" she cried.

Laughter drifted down to her, and the shoveling continued. Jessie wept with bitterness and she clung to Black Snake and felt his body take the blows. During her life, she'd been in some bad fixes, but nothing to compare with this nightmare. Soon, she thought, a large rock will strike Black Snake down and I'll fall just moments later. Drowned in hot water, buried by a demented, rock-shoveling murderer. I wish... I wish I had at least died in the sunshine, quick, with a bullet or even an arrow. Any way but this!

When Ki and the newspaper reporter jumped off the cage at the sixteen hundred foot level of the Bonanza Unlimited, the shift supervisor came hurrying up to block their progress. "Hey, you aren't allowed down here!"

Dan DeQuille did not even answer the man. He turned around in a full circle, got his compass bearings and then pointed toward a tunnel leading north. "That would be the direction we want!"

"Stop them!" the superintendent yelled to his crew.

178

By the very panic in the man's voice, Ki knew that they had found Jessie. He also knew she would be either dead or close to death and that this man was directly responsible. With a low growl in his throat, he sent the heel of his hand upward into the man's face. The nose broke, and the bones were pushed into the man's brain, killing him instantly. Then, he hobbled after DeQuille with an entire mine crew on his heels.

They snatched a lantern from the wall and hurried down the sweltering tunnel until they rounded a corner and saw a man shoveling rock from a cart into a pit.

"Stop!" Ki shouted in warning.

The man dropped his shovel and reached under his coat, clawing for a gun. Ki's own hand plucked a *shuriken* star blade out of his jacket and set it spinning through the dimly lit tunnel. The man screamed as the blade struck him in the throat. The scream died suddenly, and then he staggered and fell beside the shaft. Ki reached the pit first. "Hello!" he shouted.

Jessie sobbed with recognition of his voice. "Ki," she cried weakly. "Please get us out of here!"

Ki had no idea of who "us" might be nor did he care. All that mattered was saving Jessie's life. And yet, he knew that he would be of no help to her if he was killed. He grabbed the dead mine foreman's gun and yelled for Dan DeQuille to take cover. The newspaper reporter was no stranger to gunfights, and he raced on down the tunnel and disappeared around a corner where he would not be hit by ricocheting bullets.

Ki fired three quick shots, and the lanterns that the Bonanza crew held aloft were blown to smithereens. The mean whine of bullets careening off rock walls sent the miners scrambling back down the tunnel.

Ki heard footsteps coming from the opposite direction.

"Don't shoot!" DeQuille yelled. "It's me!"

The newspaper reporter had a couple of sticks of dynamite under one arm and a rope under the other. "I'd have gotten more but there wasn't much time. Fortunately, they're changing shifts in the Crossfire, and the station is empty."

Ki grabbed the rope and threw it down to Jessie. "Tie it around your waist," he called.

Jessie tied the rope around her waist and then gave it a sharp tug. Almost at once, she was hoisted up the slippery sides and delivered from a watery hell. Despite the fact that it was 130 degrees in the tunnel, it seemed almost cool now. She used the last of her strength to help Ki and De-Quille pull Black Snake up to the surface.

"Let's get to the Crossfire station!" Ki yelled, picking up Jessie while DeQuille helped the exhausted Black Snake down the tunnel. Angry bullets chased them north and Ki knew the Bonanza miners were coming after them.

The station was empty, but Ki knew that the cage would be down any minute. "Get ready to commandeer us four places," Ki ordered, shoving his companions toward the loading and unloading deck while he placed his lantern on the floor and jammed both sticks of dynamite into the wick's flame.

With both fuses burning, he charged the tunnel once more and shouted, "Get back! I'm going to blow this tunnel!"

The men chasing them must have seen the sparkling fuses because they errupted in shouts and reversed direction. Ki could have hurled the two sticks of dynamite into their midst, but chose not to. Instead, he pitched the dynamite about ten feet into the tunnel, then raced back to the loading platform. Looking up at the heavy square-set timbering, he said, "I hope it holds."

The cage dropped right down to them, and the startled crew of the Crossfire Mine blinked in amazement to see Jessie, Black Snake, Ki and the newspaper man all armed and shoving their way into the already crowded cage.

"It's going to blow up down here!" DeQuille yelled. "Signal the operator to take us up. Be quick!"

The miners needed no further urging. They yanked on a bell rope, and after a heart-stopping five second delay, the cage was yanked upward through the top of the huge mine station, and it soared straight up the shaft.

The explosion was awesome. Ki's two sticks of dynamite caused an entire box of dynamite resting close by to explode in a tremendous blast that actually rocked the entire Comstock Lode. Their cage banged dangerously against the sides of the shaft. A huge, billowing cloud of dust and smoke came pouring up the sides of the shaft. It overtook them at the 300 foot level and engulfed them in a choking cloud that mushroomed out of the mine and filled the entire hoisting works of the Crossfire.

Ki held onto Jessie as everyone staggered out of the mining building and ran for safety. Jessie saw Mike Colson of the Crossfire come racing out of his plush offices. "Ki, get him for me!"

The samurai unleashed a *shuriken* blade that struck the mine superintendent in the calf and dropped him in the sage, writhing in pain. Ki pulled the man erect and brought him to Jessie. "Who else?"

Jessie pointed to Dick Pardee over at the Bonanza mine. Pardee was surrounded by a big crowd of miners. "He's in on it too."

"I'll claim the pleasure of this one," Black Snake said, uncoiling his bullwhip and going after the man. Pardee saw him coming and ran. They disappeared in the sage, but

Jessie could hear the whip popping and the screams of the Bonanza Mine superintendent.

"Put up your hands!" Deputy Cutter shouted, jumping out of the crowd with a double-barreled shotgun pointed at them. "You're under arrest for murder and destruction of property! Freeze!"

Ki froze. There was no alternative. That shotgun was pointed right at them, and he knew it would rip everyone to pieces. But he also knew that, if he surrendered again, they'd never leave the Virginia City jail alive. There was just too damn much money involved for these people.

Jessie had reached the same conclusions, yet she was to weak to mount any opposition. Looking up at the sheriff, she said, "You must have the initials, D.C."

"Wrong again, Miss Starbuck, they belong to my cousin."

"Drop the shotgun, Deputy!"

Cutter spun around and would have fired if Ed hadn't killed him with a pair of bullets through the heart.

The crowd was stunned. Jessie reacted before they did. Reaching into her pocket and holding her compass and notes aloft, she faced a crowd that was starting to number in the hundreds. "People, the Bonanza and the Crossfire are joined at the sixteen hundred foot level, and maybe at all the other levels as well. These men have been manipulating stocks and making huge profits off people like yourselves."

The crowd fell silent except for one man who yelled, "Can you prove that?"

"You bet I can," Jessie answered. "I can retrace the underground tunnel if you like using these distances and angles."

"Or," Dan DeQuille said, his reach baritone voice commanding attention, "We can dispense with that, and I'll ask you men to trust me as you've always trusted me. I stand before you an honest man and the proof of that is that—as you are all well aware, I am poor, poorer even than the lowest common working man among you."

He raised his fist and shook it in Colson's face. "And I say now, and I will repeat in court, that these men have cheated us all. If we lose the trust of the thousands, perhaps even millions of investors around the world, we have nothing. And I say to you, when something is this rotten, it must be destroyed! Destroyed so that it will be known that the citizens of Virginia City will never again tolerate murder and wholesale fraud. I say we must light a couple of boxes of dynamite and drop them down the shafts of both mines!"

One miner blurted, "But . . . there's still gold down there!"

"Then start over clean and honestly!" DeQuille shouted.

Black Snake dragged Pardee through the crowd and hurled him to the dirt. "Miss Starbuck and I were left to die down there, and I swore I'd see that hell-hole covered up."

Before anyone could answer, Black Snake marched into the smoking Crossfire. He found a case of dynamite and lit one stick, then hurled the case down the shaft and took off running. Jessie felt the heat of the explosion, and then a great flume of fire came shooting up through what was left of the roof. Minutes later, someone did the same thing on the Bonanza, and as darkness fell, the twin towers of flame bathed the Comstock in an eerie light.

"There are a lot of people out here who've never had the pleasure of Circle Star beef. And they eat poorly. I'm going to drive our herd up here and donate them to those people through a charity," Jessie said, looking at the devastation." As soon as we get the sheriff and the coroner behind bars, I'm going to do that. Do it in Sarah's and Grant's name."

Ki said nothing as he stood beside the woman he had sworn to always protect. The towering flames reflected in his black eyes, and they looked to him as if someone had tapped a pair of holes into hell.